VICTOR JANE

LEGACY OF A VAMPIRE

ARTHUR JETT

ISBN
978-1-957378-66-4 (Paperback)
978-1-957378-65-7 (eBook)
978-1-957378-67-1 (Hardcover)

Victor Jane consists of three short stories about Victor, a formidable 6-foot-4 vampire seeking to kill every other "vamp" because they prey on humans.

Victor is especially intent on destroying Contessa Cortez, who murdered his family and turned him and countless others into bloodsuckers. His pure-blood Lipenstein stallion, Nightfire, accompanies Victor on his adventures as "The Cowboy Vampire," "Vampire Trucker" and "Vampire Spaceman" respectively. Because of his rare blood, Nightfire also was attacked by the Contessa. Now man and horse - both with glowing red eyes - travel the world following wars (where the undead thrive) to kill more vamps.

Along the way, Victor falls in love twice, befriends television actor/ vampire Barnaby Collingsworth (seemingly borrowed from *Dark Shadows* vampire Barnabas Collins) and kills numerous vampires and humans who conspire with them. Over eight centuries, Victor's methods adapt as technology - and his skills - advance: As a cowboy vampire, he uses Colt revolvers; as a modern-day vampire-trucker, Victor employs a deadly disrupter frequency on his CB radio; as a vampire-spaceman in 2210, he travels to planet Valgor (the origin of Earth's vampires) with a silver sword, laser pistol, light grenades, laser rifle and disrupter belt.

—Blueink Review

CONTENTS

BOOK 1
THE COWBOY VAMPIRE

BOOK 2
Vampire Trucker

BOOK 3
VAMPIRE SPACEMAN

ACKNOWLEDGMENTS

I'd like to thank my Wife, Linda, and all the Super Readers for motivating me to write this book. I would also like to thank Citizens Legal, Brenda and Pete Camren for taking on my spelling and grammar. Lastly, I'd like to thank Quantum Discovery for publishing my book.

Book One

CHAPTER ONE

ON A COLD, RAINY NIGHT just outside of Medford Oregon, the trail was dark. Like you close your eyes in a closet dark. Clouds covered the sky and moon, what little of it there was. For days the moon had been a sliver like cats eyes. It was barely noticed except by him Victor Jane, a lone cowboy with a small herd. Victor sat six feet four inches and 220 pounds. He was tall in the saddle, head hung down, chin tucked in, black hat with the brim, extra large. A black duster hung down below his knees, black pants, jean like, with black Mexican boots and Spanish spurs.

Two Colt 45 peacemakers, silver with pearl handles, hid protected from the rain under the duster. A Winchester 30/30 lever action rifle hung in the scabbard. His saddle was black, with Mexican silver inlay.

He rode a black stallion with a long mane and wide gait. The rider and horse both had eyes glowing red, as if to light the night. Yes, they could both see in the dark. Victor had always been a horseman even in the early days before he was a vampire.

Early in the 1500's his family, the Jane family had bred horses for the Army of France. France was where it had all started. Victor had taken over the day to day of running the family business of breeding horses outside of Paris.

It was one in the morning and the mare was having trouble giving birth. Victor had decided to be there, to help comfort the mare. He had an urge to sleep in the barn, because the new breed of Spanish Lipenstein would be his family's new fortune, and he was going to make sure everything was perfect.

Along with the mare came a small convoy to ensure the horse arrived in Paris safely. The convoy consisted of Senior Miguel Rojas Vargas, a slender piece of a man, bold, with dark eyes.

Also in the convoy was Miguel's wife Senora Contesa Vargas, a woman much younger than her husband. A rare beauty with black shining hair long past her shoulders, that caught every shimmering piece of light. When she looked at Victor with her big dark reddish brown eyes he felt that she was looking deep into his soul.

They had traveled here with the mare at the request of the Marquis of the Lipenstein National Equestrian Association of Spain. For the first time in a hundred years the breed had been sold, and allowed to leave Spain.

CHAPTER TWO

AT THE BIRTHING OF THE new colt, he was black and a bit hairy Victor had thought. The colt had long gangly legs, but was smart looking.

Miguel and his wife Contesa were in the barn. "We were a little an anxious to see the new colt." He explained.

As soon as the colt stood all hell broke loose. Victor watched as Miguel jumped ten feet in the air landing on the mare's throat and head. Then Miguel's face began to contort and change. In seconds he had turned into a hideous monster. His eyes became huge and blood red as if they were bleeding. His nose and nostrils flattened into a face which was now elongated by perhaps a foot. His jaw extended from his face and 4 large fangs protruded outward from his mouth. With one or two bites, Victor couldn't tell they came so fast, the monstrous creature had torn out the thrashing mare's throat and was consuming large quantities of blood with a ghoulish smile on his face. Slowly he looked around at Victor.

Within a blink of an eye Contesa had Victor by the throat. She had flickered across the floor of the barn to the wall beside the main door. Her brown eyes were now a bleeding red, her skin was a rat-like pale grey. Her once beautiful hair was now just patches of course grayish bristles. Her face was now twice as long as before, and she had claws instead of a hand that were seven inches long.

To Victor, everything was now in slow motion. Their glowing eyes were the most vivid thing in the dark, and those eyes were mostly what Victor could recall lighting the room bright red.

Jose', Victor's younger brother, burst through the door flintlock rifle in hand. He got a shot off which struck Miguel at the back of his skull. The monsters whole head exploded leaving a headless body. Contesa let out a shriek. She stopped feeding at the horses throat and leapt in one bound to Jose'. Jose' turned as if to sprint out the door just before his head fell to the ground.

Four days later Victor awoke in his bed very weak from blood loss. Bleary eyed, his chest and throat were bandaged. Then he was out again for two days. When he came to, Victor was not bleary eyed or weak but felt as if he had a long restful sleep. But sleep found him once again as if he were drunken with slumber. When he awoke next the bandages were gone and his sister and father were sitting in the room beside his bed. Victor sat up quickly.

"What happened?" he screamed.

"Lay back down my son. You should rest." His father said.

But Victors mind was working very quickly to connect the bits and pieces of memory. Small pictures were flying in and out of his mind.

His father and sister began telling him of Miguel and Contesa's rampage. How they had killed Jose' and the mare. How Victor had survived alone with the colt. Contesa was nowhere to be found. And Miguel Vargas, the best that they knew, had become dust or ash. Victor had only been slightly bitten. Jose had saved his brother at the cost of his own life.

Victor pondered that word 'saved'. "I don't think saved is the right word." He told his family.

As of that day Victor was different. It was his first consciousness as a soulless being.

CHAPTER THREE

WHEN VICTORS' FAMILY CONTACTED THE Lipenstein Equestrian Association in Spain, they were informed that their envoy had consisted of three men. None of which were Miguel or Contesa. The men had just disappeared somewhere in between Spain and France. Hijacked, eaten, and the remainder of their bodies discarded as if they were trash. The creatures were after the purebreds' blood also. This is why they let the colt live when it was born in the Jane family barn. The monsters had even used the horses as canteens of blood for their thirst along the way to France.

Victor thought about the colt and went to the barn to see him. His head seemed to boil with strange thoughts of random violence and rage under his consciousness. He rubbed his forehead again and again to push the feelings back, but it was no good. Whatever these feelings were, they were taking over.

When the colt first saw Victor he tried to scramble back. The colt was frightened and it was clear he sensed something in this tall man. Gently Victor moved closer to him. Slowly he stroked the black hair of the horses' mane and whispered it would be okay.

In only a few days Victor was raging with hunger that was ever present within him. Leaving was the only thing he could think of to do. He feared for the safety of his father and sister. The feelings were so great that he just ran, and ran. Through the night, a day, and then the next night.

The smell of water first hit his nostrils then Victor heard the sound. Then he heard the beating of a heart, a human heart. As if by an inborn animal nature he was upon the human. Fright gripped the peasant. He could not move. In one swift motion Victor had opened the man's artery. Blood was gushing and Victor was lapping, chewing, and licking at it. Delirious, euphoric, as Victor dropped the body to the ground, he felt exhausted with pleasure, and the fulfillment of his kill. Then he heard the scream.

"Vampire!!" A gypsy woman ran from the stream yelling, "Vampire, vampire!"

Who was she screaming about? Victor had not seen a vampire. But he had! Contesa!

Victor realized she had bitten him, but he had not reciprocated and feasted on her blood. Suddenly he realized that the musket blast that had splattered Miguel's head into pieces must have gotten into his own mouth. Now it had begun to turn him into a vampire.

With a frightening burst of speed Victor was in front of the gypsy woman, still smeared with the blood of his kill. With both hands on her shoulders he demanded of her, "Stop screaming! Now tell me all you know of vampires!" Which she did. For the next year Victor traveled with the gypsy band learning to live with what he was. He became a part of the sideshow for the gypsies and town folk. And they moved from town to town.

CHAPTER FOUR

A YEAR HAD PASSED. THE traveling show was back outside of Paris, close to Victors home. The feelings that had come with his condition, or infection, were under control. Well, at least he hadn't eaten anyone for months. Plus he wanted to see his father and sister.

They must have been worried sick over his disappearance. Victor had not stopped thinking of the black colt. As he approached the house he saw the young horse in the pasture. He must have sensed Victor because his head went high in the air as he stood regally. Not shy or frightened as when it was a foal.

"Victor! Victor!" it was his sister Jewels. "Victor you're home! Finally you're home! I knew you would come back!" She yelled as she threw herself into his arms, "I missed you. I am so glad you're home!"

After a few moments, Victor asked Jewels where father was. Her demeanor changed quickly, "Father is gone", she said.

Her eyes looked to the ground. "Two days after you left his heart just stopped from sadness over Jose' being killed and you gone missing. She then pointed at our family cemetery where the newer markers had been erected.

"It had been so hard with all of you being gone, but I have managed. Mostly by selling livestock. All but Nightfire, the black stallion colt" she said. "I just couldn't sell him."

"You named him?" Victor asked.

"Yes because of the firestorm the night he was born" she replied.

"I see", Victor managed to say.

The next two years were spent training Nightfire, who Victor felt a strong bond with. But time was flying by. The two years seemed only moments to Victor, as if from morning to dusk in one day.

Jewels and Victor talked of the night their lives where changed forever. His condition was complete now. He could not withstand any direct sunlight. His body must be covered from any and all sunlight, especially the eyes. Spectacles had to be worn in the day light, so most of the training for Nightfire was at night with lamps. Still Victor had to eat. Goats, rats and cattle were fine as long as he killed them. If not he ran the risk of infecting them and having them turn. He didn't want the neighboring farmers goat catching fire in the daylight.

Still what felt like seconds to him were months to Jewels. The colt was almost five now. Victor had started to sense others overhead, passing within a mile or so. Other vamps. That's what he called them.

He rode the big black horse back to his gypsy friends. Nightfire was very smart and learned quickly. This was the best trained horse Victor had ever seen. Giovanni Luigi was the husband of the gypsy Rosa that had brought Victor to them. Victor was very much like family to them. They were amazed with Nightfire. Giovanni and his band of gypsies often stayed on the outskirts of the Jane family farm, even though the only family left was Jewels and Victor.

One night Victor said to Giovanni, "I sense we are not alone. There are many vamps." Giovanni agreed. He had seen evidence of this also. Two gypsies had gone missing from a trip into town just outside of Paris. Giovanni had informed the police but nothing was ever done. One of Giovanni's best horses had to be put down because he had become infected and was turning vampire.

CHAPTER FIVE

AS VICTOR RETURNED HE COULD sense something was wrong at his farm. Something was very, very wrong. He spurred Nightfire into running as fast as he could go. Still to Victor this was like slow motion. He leaped from the horse and started running many times faster than the horse. At home the house was in total disarray. A huge struggle had taken place. There was blood everywhere. He looked around and fear gripped what soul he had retained. Jewels was hanging upside down pinned to the kitchen wall stripped of clothes and most of her skin. What had been fear was now eternal rage for vamps!!!

Outside there was a large commotion. In an instant he was outside beheading the first vamp bare handed. As he turned a second vamp just nicked him. As he pulled away Victor fell on his neck and decapitated him. An amber flash, then dust and ash all that was left of the two.

A third vampire leapt from Nightfire where she had been feasting. She landed on Victor full force knocking almost unconscious. "You belong to me Victor" the creature screeched. Suddenly as she started to bite down a mighty kick came from Nightfire sending the vamp flying, tumbling through the air. This gave Victor the time to recover, but it was too late. The vamp was gone.

Victor buried Jewels next to his father and Jose'. On their graves he swore an oath to kill all vampires by any means.

He attended to Nightfire's wounds but it did not look good for the black stallion. The wounds were deep and infection was setting in. Giovanni and his wife had come to help but it was too late. Jewels was gone and Nightfire, who had saved him was lying at deaths door.

Giovanni said to him, "Victor you must destroy your horse or turn him into a vampire as yourself."

Victor howled a deafening shriek. He loved that black stallion! So he sliced his own arm wide and deep then put it-in Nightfire's mouth. Nothing happened at first but then the horse drank wildly until he pulled his arm away. Almost immediately the big black Lipenstein stallion arose with force and walked to Victor as if to ask, "Shall we go?"

CHAPTER SIX

IT WAS THE YEAR SIXTEEN twelve. It had also been almost one hundred years later and hundreds of vamps had been sent to hell. The rider and horse could flash through the countryside in the blink of an eye. The big black stallion was now ten times as strong as before and Victor's killing skill had been honed to perfection. He had commissioned carved wooden balls with crosses for his musket. Victor also now had a long saber sword made of pure silver from Spain, especially for cutting heads off vamps. Nightfire's long black hair coat protected his flesh from the sunlight, but his eyes nose and mouth had to be covered with a mask, as did Victors body, face, and eyes. At night their eyes could light the entire night. Perfect for searching for vamps, their favorite thing to do. It really was their whole life and purpose.

The vampire mind ran rampant for their next feast or kill, and the unholy mayhem which always ensued. And for this reason, as best Victor could tell, the vamps did not sense him or the black stallion. Maybe they just sensed a brother vampire. Whatever it was Victor always seemed to have the jump on them.

Some of them would be flying above him, or flicker by him moving so fast that the human eye could not see or would not see. Victor saw the vamps as a light gray or brown movement. For some reason they could be within a quarter of a mile or so and not sense him. But this was plenty close for Victor and Nightfire to run them down and grab them. The wooden stake, and beheading were Victor's favorite. Sometimes they would be stomped by Nightfire until they turned to dust or ash, and just floated away. Most vamps looked like vamps. Some are more sophisticated, human-like, and much more dangerous.

The older, much wiser and very elusive ones; it always gave great pleasure to Victor to kill one of these vamps. Contesa was one of these vamps. It was over two hundred years since he had seen her last. Could she be dead in the sense of the word, turned to dust and ash? He hoped not. But still, all must die, and he had travelled searching most of Europe, from France east. The vamps were now very scared. That made them harder to find and those who knew of the legend avoided his path by hundreds of miles, cities, and now countries away. Still Victor had vowed, they all must die.

The vamps would hide in war! They could feast and no one would notice them in their atrocity! Blending in was the way to go now, at least for the smart ones. No more just plucking them out of the air. Victor knew that if there was a particularly bloody battle the vamps would be close, and so would he and the black stallion. More often than not vamps travelled in covens or packs. If a blitz would hit a town or city, more than likely vamps were close to reap the benefits. In war zones they moved fast, stopping only to finish the wounded, sucking the final life from the nearly dead, panicked humans.

In areas where the plague was, it would be the vamps themselves spreading the plague. Bad blood did not affect them as long as their victims were still alive.

Yes the vamps were getting smarter. They were more adept at staying incognito. But Victor had started out blessed with above average intelligence, and learned more with each passing generation. He attending a montage of schools, universities, entering a sword apprenticeship, and gun making machinists. He became a master of war and weaponry. Because Victor did not age he of course moved regularly. Five years here, two years there. He seemed to get along with humans just fine. After all he had to eat, but not like vamps. And, all vamps must die.

Humans, for the most part were good. But then some were bad. Really bad. Most humans did not know about vamps, or if they did know they chose not to believe it until it was too late. There were also those who helped the vampires. In Victor's book they were no better than a vamp and they also must die.

Hence they become food for Victor and for Nightfire. Most of the time a lamb slaughtered over the grass was fine for Nightfire. Or maybe a chicken beheaded over his feed worked also. He was a vampire after all with all their abilities and drawbacks. In fact, in all the years Victor had been a vampire the black stallion was the only thing that he had ever turned into a vampire. That was only because he loved the horse so much. He could not lose the only being that he felt understood him. Everyone else was dead. Jewels, Father, Jose', the band of gypsies, Giovanni and his wife. All were long dead.

Victor had heard of the New World. In the Americas, it was said, a man could be free and there was plenty of land for all. After two hundred and fifty years crisscrossing Europe it was just about time for a change. Victor made his way to Muenster, Germany and booked a passage, first class of course, for himself and his black Lipenstein stallion. The ship slowly made its way along the rivers and canals to the North Sea. Then they transferred to an ocean vessel.

Victor had given the captain orders that only he himself would feed and water his horse. Seeing that the horse was high strung the captain understood. Besides it would be less trouble for him. Victor did not want to have to explain his horse eating a sailor.

Eighteen forty on February the sixth they landed in New York harbor. It was gray, cold, and snowy which is how Victor liked it, dark and damp. He did not have to be covered from the sunlight as much, but it was never a surety.

They stayed in New York for a short time. It didn't take long to find a large coven of vamps. Victor had set out to kill them all. As he was doing reconnaissance on the vamps lair he discovered something very interesting.

Victor captured two vampires and a human sympathizer. He just wanted information. The first vamp, was a skinny red head that had not turned all the way. His human nose was missing and ears were a bit pointed with a few patches of wiry red hair.

Victor demanded "Tell me of your pack!"

The red head vamp just hissed and said, "I will tell you nothing!"

Victor pulled his saber from its sheath slowly and with one stroke sliced off the red headed vamps head.

The human started crying out "I know where she keeps them!"

Victor turned as the second vamp spoke, "Shut up you fool!"

Victor placed the silver sword to the vamps heart, and again slowly pushed it into the creature's heart. A quick flame, then ash, and finally dust, all in just a moment.

The human's eyes were as big as silver dollars. He shook with fright and said, "Mister those vampires can make you live forever. Is that what you want with them?"

Victor looked at the human and said, "Where does she keep them?"

He responded, "I can show you."

Victor put the saber to the human's throat, "Where is she?" Victor asked.

"Behind the Red Door Saloon hidden under the hotel. There are a lot of vampires there mister, and they will eat you without someone like me." Victor's eyes glowed bright red. His face began to change from human to vampire.

He said, "Or maybe *I* will eat **them**."

The man started to scream, but with a snip from the sword he was no more than a human straw.

CHAPTER SEVEN

AS VICTOR AND NIGHTFIRE APPROACHED the waterfront, they both sensed the vamps. A few went overhead, and to Victors surprise they seemed to slow a bit. As if they were wondering what it was that made them feel uneasy.

Victor said to Nightfire, "Huh, that's new." Then he nudged the horse forward.

As they stopped in front of the saloon, Victor noticed blood along the boardwalk. Not a lot. It was muddy and if you were not a vampire you would not know it was there. Music came from inside. Victor stepped down from the big stallion. Nightfire snorted loudly as if to say, "I am coming too".

Victor calmed him and said, "Stay big fellow". Then he laid the reins on the hitching post. Not tied just laid.

Laughter and conversations became louder as Victor pushed the swinging door open. The laughter and conversations quickly stopped. The room was filled with smoke, the smell of whiskey, stale beer, sweat, dirt, and the unmistakable smell of vamp, which was a lot like rat dung.

Victor counted nine altogether, six humans and three vamps. Victor stopped at the end of the bar. The bartender slowly walked down to where Victor stood. He said curtly, "Mister this here is a private club. You will have to leave." He blew out smoke from his cigar.

"Now that's not very friendly of you." Victor responded, "All I wanted was a shot of red eye, and yours will do just fine."

Before the smoke could curl again Victor plucked out both the barkeep's eyes, and started chewing them up. All hell broke loose, but Victor had played it all out before the doors had stopped swinging. The Colt 45 on his left hip shot five times, and the one on his right hip fired three times. It was the one with wooden slugs for bullets. Two of them struck the vamps on the other end of the bar. In the slow commotion Victor had thought to himself, "Flame on vamps!", as ash flew and dust fell.

As for the five humans, they had all gone for their guns. They were all dead, most of them before they hit the floor. Victor reloaded, lead for the left and wood for the right. He walked slowly toward the back of the saloon. The smoke from the 45's was thick. It swirled around Victor like an ominous gray cloud of magic.

He sensed movement. He spoke out "Is that you Contesa?"

"It is I Victor. Here I am. I am your worst nightmare. Do you remember? I am your..."

At that moment gunfire rang out from the second floor. One bullet hit Victor above his left collar bone, knocking him backward into the wall hard. In a blink of his eyes he fired two shots, catching two vamps who now were half way across the room in midair. The dust sprayed around him. A shot came again from the second floor. This one missed. Instantly Victor was standing there next to the human, who had fired it. His eyes grew large and his face turned pale. Victor knew there was plenty of blood to be had. With his claw-like hand Victor grabbed the bottom of the mans Adam's Apple and ripped upwards toward his nose. The bottom jaw was unhinged and the blood flowed like a fountain. Victor drank and did not mind it at all. The human fell. At that he wiped his mouth and yelled, "Contesa!"

Most of the waterfront should have heard him. Victor could now hear Nightfire kicking and destroying the saloon, Victor quickly mounted the black stallion, and rode fast into the night. He could not sense if it was her or not, but whoever she was, she was gone.

CHAPTER EIGHT

THERE WERE PLENTY OF VAMPS in New York, and more arriving every day from all over the world. Europe, China, Russia, Africa, and they all must die. Victor spent the next few days looking for any information on Contesa he could find, which was not much.

A somewhat classic lady with auburn hair, dark eyes, and had been doing her entertaining at night. She went by the name, Countess Contesa Silva Cortez. But she was gone now. Disappeared. There was no scent of her at all. Victor was upset with himself for letting her get away, so he took it out on the new arrivals.

As they flickered off the incoming ships to the New York harbor Victor would pick them off one by one. Mostly he used his sword or sometimes a wooden stakes through the heart. Those that leapt from the ship could be taken out with his long rifle. It was some of the easiest hunting ever, although it was noisy.

Eventually he even tired of this but he wanted Contesa Cortez on the blade of his sword. So Victor and Nightfire left New York and headed south, down the coast into Virginia and the Carolinas. Not a lot of vamps, but they would pop up now and then. It did not ever take much for Victor to find them. They were bold to say the least. They had no natural enemies, with the exception of Victor and Nightfire, and it was a big world. Only Contesa would ever think of Victor and the black stallion as an enemy.

What Victor did see was more variety of vamps. They were starting to blend in with humans. More and more they could hold their human shape and control their lust for blood. So Victor had to be more careful. He did not want to kill humans...well, unless they were bad. And there were plenty of those, bad humans. Bad to other humans, like making them slaves. Beating, killing, and raping women. This seemed more common in the South, but it was true all over. The bad ones he allowed himself to use for dinner.

Charleston, South Carolina eighteen sixty, and the sun had just set. Nightfire slowly wandered toward a small livery. There Victor would get the big black stallion cleaned. Oats, hay, and they shared the blood of a rabbit Victor had shot earlier. A short skinny man came out of the livery.

"Can I help you mister?" He asked.

Victor said, "A stall for my horse, oats, and hay if you got it."

"Sure mister that will be four bits a day", responded the short man.

"Okay," Victor said, "He has been under the weather lately. I will take care of him myself."

"Sure mister", the skinny man said, "He sure is a good looking horse"

"Thanks", Victor replied, "I just need somewhere quiet until he feels better."

"Alright", the skinny man responded.

Afterwards Victor walked through the streets of Charleston trying to get a feel for vamps. A particularly strong feeling came from the saloon.

Victor crossed in from the dark of night to the dim light of the saloon. There was some low talk and then none. They were all human. Victor walked to the bar. "Bottle" he said. The bar keeper looked at him and brought over a bottle.

"That will be a dollar cowboy", the bartender barked.

Victor slapped it down on the bar, grabbed the bottle, and went to a corner table, laying his long rifle on the table top. Victor did not really need the bottle. It was just his way of blending in. That way he could find out about the vamps. Saloons were a favorite place to feed; easy kills, usually in the alleys in the dark. Victor just needed the scent of a vamp to do his killing. He didn't have long to wait.

In walked a vamp, fancy clothes and all. His suite was tailor made. Pearl handled six shooter, a bowler hat, button down lapels, and a fancy walking cane. Vamp alright, pale skin, eyes a bit sunken, big happy grin, and not a care in the world. That was until he saw Victor in the corner. His stride slowed immediately. His head seemed to turn back slowly towards the bar, like he had seen something very bad that he did not want to see. He ordered a whiskey.

"Have some of mine." Victor said from the corner. The vamp smiled as he turned toward Victor. "Why thank you." he said. "And may I join you?"

"Please do", Victor replied as he kicked the chair out a little from the table. "Barkeep a glass please."

The vamp walked to the table, sat down, and poured himself a drink as if he and Victor had been lifelong friends. "Thank you sir. My name is Barnaby Collingsworth. I am from Boston. Who might you be?"

Victor found this very amusing, a vamp socializing with him. "My name is Victor Jane. I'm from Paris." He said.

"Well Victor, I run a small import export business here in Charleston. Mostly items from Europe, and I export cotton and sugar from the local plantations. It's very profitable, and I enjoy travelling abroad so as to see my clientele. What about you Victor Jane? What do you do?" He asked.

"I am a horseman. I breed very fine horses. And I also hunt, and kill vampires much like yourself Barnaby." Victor said.

"I thought as much, the killing that is. Imagine my surprise when I first saw you. The reason you haven't killed me yet is because you want to know if I know anything about Contesa Cortez." He stated.

Victor's grip tightened on the pistol he had gripped under the table and he brought the gun to the top of the table. "Why yes Barnaby that is exactly why I did not kill you."

"Good we can work a deal!" Barnaby said loudly smiling.

Victor responded hesitantly with "We surely can Barnaby. We surely can."

Barnaby proceeded quietly. "There are vampires and lots of them. They are infecting the slaves, and that is affecting cotton productivity. It's Contesa Cortez that is infecting them. Contesa is truly out of control. Just from her frenzy she is building a small mindless vampire army, and in turn they are infecting whole regions of villages and towns through South Carolina. I have tried to eradicate them myself, but there are too many." The vamp sounded sincere.

"Where are they now? I don't get a sense they are here." Victor said skeptically.

"But as a matter of fact they're fifty miles south of here. Their numbers are growing like a wildfire raging out of control. I'll help you get Contesa Cortez. You help me to clean out the vampires?" Barnaby suggested with his dazzling grin.

Victor did not trust the vamp, but he was curious. Where he had come from? Where did he stay? Victor needed more information, so for the moment Barnaby would live. Victor now sensed other vampires nearby. Victor said, "When do we leave?".

The vamp responded, "I have a small piece of business to attend to tonight."

"And what might that be?" asked Victor.

"Just some provisions for a plantation of mine, but I must hurry. The whole sunlight thing makes me nervous. Although my carriage is especially constructed to shield its passengers from the sunlight, I'm sure you know what I mean." Barnaby said.

"Yes I do. I will accompany you." Victor said. "That is of you don't mind."

"Surely. Suit yourself." Barnaby responded. So the two were up and out of the saloon without an incident. Not the norm for Victor.

It was late and Barnaby had made arrangements with the shop keep to make some purchases. Flour, whiskey, some books, and cloth to make clothing. Victor was diligent in watching Barnaby for any wrong move. His senses were on high alert around other vampires. Actually Victor trusted no one, especially vamps.

"Shall we go quickly Barnaby? I must stop at the livery for my horse." Victor stated.

"For your horse?" Barnaby asked, alarmed, "It will be daylight before we arrive at my home."

"Do not worry about it." Victor said, and motioned with his hand as if to say, "After you?"

A large black man in a very fine suit, top hat, and big white carnation on his lapel sat upon what looked like a stage coach. It was well built, black with wooden shutters on it drawn by four horses perfectly matched. As Barnaby opened the door a faint light shined through the door. Curtains of red crushed velvet covered the doorway. Barnaby disappeared inside then his head came back out and said, "I will meet you at Jones and Co. Mercantile. Its two blocks up on the left."

Victor walked to the livery trying to get a sense of any vamps or just bad humans, but nothing. And that made Victor extremely wary.

CHAPTER NINE

VICTOR RODE UP TO THE Jones Mercantile just as Barnaby and his colleague, the driver, came out with arms full of supplies. Barnaby said, "Nice horse Mr. Jane." Victor loved his horse, but a "nice horse"? Victor grinned to himself thinking, "Yes if he's not eating you." Which was not a bad idea?

Barnaby's driver was not a vampire or in a trance as sometimes happened to humans. What was it then? Just a job for his master, or was his ambition more lofty? The carriage headed south out of Charleston. After riding through the day into the night, Barnaby appeared from the carriage grinning as usual, "Good evening Victor. It is amazing that you have survived, but yet there you are. What is your secret?"

Victor ignored Barnaby. "How much further?"

Barnaby replied smiling. "We will be there before daylight."

Still no sense of vamps, except Barnaby. 'Beware!' Victor thought to himself, for it had been awhile since Victor had rested. Not that he needed much rest since becoming a vamp. He could, and others did stay awake for days. Usually in a dark cool place, but still it was more human to sleep than vamp.

The carriage continued south-west. Soon flickers of vamps were passing over them, and in the distance there was "normal" vamp movement. As the black carriage turned from the main road Victor could see a large house a half mile ahead. The small pea gravel road leading to the house was lined with moss covered weeping willow trees. Wind blew gently making them look like soft waves rolling above the roadway, as if one were under a green beach.

The carriage came to a stop in front of the house. The place seemed old, and there was less than ten feet distance to the porch. The porch was lined with a few Roman style columns. The house was two stories with a large second floor balcony.

Barnaby spoke, "Home sweet home".

His servant greeted them. "So glad you home mister Collingsworth", the servant said.

Almost as if he really had missed him.

Barnaby yelled up at the driver, "Please put Mr. Jane's horse in the stable..."

Victor cut him off saying, "I would prefer doing it myself."

"As you wish Victor." said Barnaby.

At the stable Victor asked, "What is your name?" to the driver.

"Jedediah Johnson sir." he answered, "But most people call me Jed."

Victor instructed him, "Jed, my horse is high strung. Make sure he is not disturbed, and he is to be left alone."

"Yes sir", Jed said.

Victor began tending the black stallion. He cleaned, fed, and watered him.

Then Victor followed Jed and together they entered the house from the rear entrance. It lead to a small boot room where they cleaned their boots. They then moved through the kitchen where a large black woman was at work fixing food for breakfast. The smell of chicken and bacon filled the house. It must be for the help, Victor thought.

Victor carried his saddle bag on his shoulder through a dining room into a study where Barnaby stood by a fire. "Jed, show Mr. Jane to his room so he may freshen up and rest. I will see you this evening Victor. Let's say just after dark?" Barnaby asked.

"Where exactly are we Barnaby?" Victor said with a cautious voice.

Barnaby replied, smiling as usual, "Adams Run, but we will talk this evening."

"Of course." Victor said.

The house was well kept. Not like vampires, but open, airy, and alive. More like humans. The hall to his room was lined with portraits of men and some of women, all very striking. The day passed in a blink of an eye. No vamps, but the white noise of humans moving about. A bath was drawn in a room connecting to Victor's as the sun went down.

Jed appeared, "Clean clothing for you to wear Mr. Jane while I see to yours."

"Thanks Jed." Victor said. The hot bath was really a treat.

"Barnaby will be in the parlor waiting for you when you are ready sir."

"Thank you Jed. Tell Mr. Collingsworth I will be there soon." Victor said.

Barnaby was waiting in the parlor and greeted him with a smile. "Victor, you are finally here!", He exclaimed with gusto as he entered the room, "Would you like some whiskey or perhaps red wine?"

"Wine will be fine." Not necessary, Victor thought, but for appearances why not? Somehow Victor was glad he had not killed Barnaby yet. He wanted to see how all of this would play out. Also, Victor had not allowed anybody into his world in over three hundred lonely years.

At that moment Victor sensed movement of another human as she entered. "Oh Barnaby! Brother you are home!" And a woman greeted him with a loving embrace. She saw Victor and said, "Oh I am sorry I did not know you had company."

"Kendra this is Mr. Jane. He will be staying with us for a while I hope. Victor, this is my sister Kendra."

Victor felt his heart stop. She was the most beautiful woman he had ever seen. He could not help himself. He had not felt such feelings in over three hundred and fifty years, and wondered how it was possible. She had golden spun hair which caught light like diamonds. Her smooth creamy skin was flawless, and she had dark blue sapphire eyes that seemed to look into the soul.

She walked over to Victor held out her hand and said, "It's a pleasure to meet you Mr. Jane."

"You may call me Victor", he said taking her hand.

"I shall do that Victor." she replied with a smile.

Her voice sent warmth through his ageing soul or what was left of it. He had looked twenty-five years old for centuries, never getting older in flesh. And now Kendra made him feel twenty-five again, she was magnificent.

She turned to Barnaby, "I'm sorry I was not in when you came home, but Mrs. Albright has been ill and I was tending her. I'm afraid the poor dear may not make it. Did you pick up the provisions I asked for?"

"Yes my dear, I did. Jed! Could you please bring the package to Miss Kendra?"

"I must return to her soon. Victor would you care to join me?" she asked.

"Well, yes. Of course." Victor responded grinning.

"Kendra, Victor and I have some business to discuss..." Barnaby interjected.

"I'm sure Victor would not mind, would you?" Kendra interrupted.

"Why, I would not mind at all." Victor responded.

The two left Barnaby standing in his study with a confused look on his face.

Her carriage was still rigged up. She placed the package in the back and said, "Shall we go Victor?"

Victor climbed aboard the buggy and took the reins. Right at the end of the path the moon was starting to come up. It was almost a full moon and her hair reflected it as if pieces had fallen into her hair. Stars shined in her eyes. Victor could hear her heart beat racing and felt her warmth through her skin.

"It's not too far." She said. Just then Victor felt a sharp pain in his back. The sting of an arrow, he gasped and fell forward and Kendra pulled him back. She took the reins and galloped the team at a full stride. What Victor had thought to be an arrow was actually a gunshot that had left a small hole in his back. A human would have been dead by now.

CHAPTER TEN

VICTOR AWOKE THE NEXT DAY. He was in bed and there beside him in a chair was Kendra Collingsworth. She had been there the whole time. "What happened?" Victor said very softly.

Kendra told him he had been shot, but she did not know who had done it. The shot had come from far way. She hadn't even heard the report. The wound was very bad, but it had almost healed. The bullet had made a little hole where it had entered, and a larger exit hole just under Victor's collar bone. He did not heal instantly, but a couple of days he would be like new.

She looked directly at Victor and said fearfully, "You are like Barnaby... a vampire."

He said looking away, "Yes, I am a vampire. But I am different. I hunt vampires. That is what I do. I am here to rid the countryside of vampires. That's why Barnaby brought me here."

"Are you also going to kill Barnaby?" she asked.

"I thought I was but now I don't know. He is different." Victor thought a moment. "Like me in a way."

Kendra asked, "What made you any better?"

"I am not." Victor said, "Well not until I met you Kendra."

"I feel the same way Victor. Ever since I first saw you I knew you would be the only one for me." Kendra said. He pulled her close to him and she leaned in to kiss him. "If Barnaby believes, then I believe also that you can save us all from the madness that is here Victor." She whispered.

"How could I not succeed with you at my side strengthening me." Victor whispered.

He kissed her again, as deep as three hundred and fifty years of waiting would allow.

Kendra attended Victor and Mrs. Albright. That evening Barnaby arrived. "He lives thanks to you sis," He grinned expansively, "but we must find out who shot him! He said more seriously. "Not many guns around here that can shoot that far and do that much damage." Barnaby observed.

Barnaby was an excellent hunter who along with Kendra had hunted with their father and mother, who also had loved to hunt. Being a good shoot was part of the culture here.

Victor felt strange that the only vamp he could sense was Barnaby. "How long?" Victor asked?

"How long what?" Barnaby replied.

"How long have you been a vampire Barnaby?" Victor said.

"Going on three years. I was attacked while on my way home from Charleston one night. As I rode along something struck my horse and me. I must have been unconscious for a moment, because the next thing I knew I was staring at a monster feeding upon my mount. It was eating the flesh. It wasn't aware I had stood, and pulled my pistol, but before I could fire it had leaped from the horse to me.'

'As I fell back the gun went off, but the creature had already begun to feed on me. There was blood everywhere. The horse had not died right away, but the stallion bled like a river, then he mercifully died. When my gun went off the bullet hit the vampire in the face and part of his head was blown away. Jed found me two days later wandering the road not far from where it all happened, feverish out of my head.'

'He took me home and cleaned me up, but it was not long after that when I started to change. My skin would blister and catch fire if it was expose to direct sunlight. I healed very quickly. I thirsted for flesh and blood. I was out of control. My first kill was a young slave girl from the plantation. Afterward my rage subsided but a vague reality of my horrible crime remained. It was not so vivid, but I remembered somewhat. So I tried cows, sheep, pigs, and rodents; anything but humans to satisfy the hunger, and control my emotion, the rage." Barnaby replied.

Victor was puzzled by what Barnaby said. Perhaps it was he himself who was still weak.

Barnaby returned home leaving Victor in Kendra's care. After one more day Victor was up and about. Kendra seemed pleased about this, but somewhat sad too. Victor could not put his finger on it so he would leave it alone for the moment. He enjoyed being with her, the way she smelled, her southern drawl; her world filled his empty soul. Her beauty made him feel alive. Like he hadn't been afflicted with the vampire curse.

Victor walked up to the second floor where Kendra had been seeing to Mrs. Albright. Her family had been one of the first in South Carolina. Victor knocked on her half opened door. Kendra said, "Oh Victor please come in I have someone special I would like you meet."

"Yes, Victor come in. I want to meet you. Kendra has been talking my ear off about you young man." Mrs. Albright was a frail woman. White hair, maybe a hundred pounds, in her late sixties Victor thought.

"How do you do ma'am? Are you feeling better?" Victor asked.

"Yes much better thanks to Kendra. She has been wonderful. Keeping me cool when the fever hit. Oh and feeding me with her great cooking! A fine trait in a woman wouldn't you say Victor?" Mrs. Albright stated.

"Why yes ma'am, a very fine quality." Victor responded.

Kendra turned two shades of red and said, "Oh stop. You two you are making me blush!"

"Victor from where is that accent I hear? From France maybe?" asked Mrs. Albright.

"Yes madam, I am from France. I was raised just outside of Paris." Victor said.

"Call me Heidi please. Aah Paris! I was there as a young child with my parents. I don't recall much of it, but I do remember them being very happy." Mrs. Albright said.

Victor turned to Kendra then said, "I must return to the plantation Kendra. The business with Barnaby."

"Oh you two run along now. I will be fine." Mrs. Albright interjected.

"Okay. I will be back to check on you tomorrow." Kendra said, grinning slyly at Victor.

Kendra and Victor had not said anything about Victor being shot. Barnaby had brought Victors clothing so it was like nothing had happened.

Kendra held on tight as they drove the buggy back to the Adams Run.

"Oh Victor I am worried about you and Barnaby." Kendra stated. Someone was trying to kill him, and she knew it. Victor ran the team of horses to the front of the mansion, lifted her gently out of it, and held her in his arms.

"Kendra my darling, there is nothing for you to worry about." Victor said, then kissed her for a long time. When he stopped he said, "I would not let you or Barnaby be hurt in any way."

"But Victor how could this possibly work for us? I am not a vampire and you are over three hundred years old, living off human blood! And yet after only a few days I know that you are the only one for me." Kendra wondered aloud.

He kissed her again passionately. Suddenly, abruptly they were pulled apart. "What are you two doing?!" It was Barnaby and he was furious. "**HE** is a vampire and for God's sake **SHE** is my baby sister!" Barnaby yelled.

"Barnaby please! I love him!" Kendra said while she grabbed his arm. "Please Barnaby can't you see I will die without him!"

"What kind of spell have you put upon her Victor?! Release her from it! You know our rage, our *hunger*, our *EVIL*! She is pure and that is good! I will not stand for it!" Barnaby raged.

Victor knew Barnaby was right.

"Victor let us go away from here." Kendra said crying reaching for him.

He moved toward her. As he did a rifle crack sounded and suddenly she stopped crying. Her eyes went wide looking at Victor. She collapsed in his arms. "Victor my love." She whispered. And then she was gone.

The bullet had missed its mark, intended for Victor. From far away a man stood out from behind the barn. Victor was on him in a second. It was Jed, holding a long rifle. "***What have you done***?!" Victor screamed, "***Why have you done this***?!"

"I could not let you take her from me. I loved her! She was as my own, like my daughter! The only thing I had left. Now she is gone too!" Jed said. Crying with fear and grief he fell to his knees.

Victor turned for a moment to look back at Kendra and Barnaby. There was a popping report of a pistol and Jed fell to the ground before Victor could stop him. Barnaby was holding Kendra in his arms. Her beaming light of life was gone. He sobbed. "She was the only thing that held me to the human world Victor. The only good thing."

Victor knelt down and touched her hair. "It is true Barnaby, love conquers all. She had brought me back to life." Victor said.

"It is all my fault!" Barnaby cried out through tears. "The slave girl I murdered was Jed's child! Gena and Kendra grew up together. When Gena was killed by me Jed lost his mind from grief as shall I!"

He leaned over and kissed Kendra's face.

Victor buried Kendra and Jed on a hill overlooking Adams Run. Barnaby sat for three days and nights. When he came to Victor he seemed rejuvenated and resolved. "We must go. We must kill all the vampires Victor! My sisters' death must not be for naught." Barnaby said, and Victor agreed. That evening the pair set out for Savanna.

CHAPTER ELEVEN

THE TWO VAMPIRES RODE TOWARD Savanna. Victor upon the big black Lipenstein stallion, and Barnaby on a pure bred Arabian Grey Carol, a magnificent horse. Barnaby's father had brought some stock from Arabia on a trip to Egypt. They had bred over twenty head, a few to sell, but mostly for the family.

Barnaby and Victor hadn't talked much. "I am sorry Victor, about Kendra I mean. She loved you. I could see it in her eyes and felt it from her heart." Barnaby said from behind. He brought up his horse next to Victor and said, "I was wrong about you and her."

Victor just looked at Barnaby then back down to the ground with a blank stare. "That bullet was meant for me, but instead it put out the light of my world. And you weren't wrong Barnaby. Jed was not wrong for trying to stop me." Neither of them had any anger for Jed, only sorrow.

The two dark figures rode through the night. Savanna was a four day ride. Barnaby did not do well in the sunlight. So in the daylight he would go into a heavy canvas tent. Or into the darkest places they could find until at dusk he could ride again.

They both had differences in their vampire powers. More a curse than powers, Victor had often thought. Barnaby's senses were not as keen as Victors. Victor could sense a vamp moving up to a mile away and most vamps could not sense him at all, but both of them were fast and strong. Barnaby had a lot of control over his hunger and rage, whereas Victor had not so much. It was kill and maybe ask questions later for Victor. Barnaby had always been a very good hunter, good with a rifle. Victor had had to learn how to be a killer, master of the sword and pistol. Both could rip a man apart. After all they were vampires.

About fifteen miles out of Savanna, Victor started getting heavy vibrations of vampire movement around them and overhead. They seemed preoccupied as usual, but it still made the horses uneasy.

Barnaby observed, "We are getting close now."

There had been a lot of murders and people going missing in Savanna for months. Little did the good folks of Savanna know they were being feasted upon in rich fashion by vampires.

It was getting close to daylight. Barnaby would have to stop before reaching the town and go into the dark. Victor would do some reconnaissance of Savanna. This way he could get a feel for the vamps; to smell them out where they lingered in force.

At dusk Victor returned to the camp where Barnaby was just moving around. He stepped from the tent and said, "Ah Victor, you are here." Always the smile. No feeling, no sense of Victor at all. He just did not have it or it was not developed in him yet. With this lack of sense, vamps could attack him without him feeling it coming.

Victor had to remember this. There was going to be a fight. No not even a fight but a battle, and three hundred and fifty years of lessons of war had served him well. But they must die! All vampires must die!

"There is a hotel on the north side of town. It has a saloon. That is where the vamps are nesting. I could smell them two blocks away."

"That bad huh?" Barnaby spoke in a low voice. Somewhat unsure of what was next.

Victor started checking his pistols. "We'll wait awhile then go and have ourselves a drink. What do you think Barnaby?"

"Sure Victor. I am a bit parched myself." Barnaby said, as he loaded his new Henry repeating rifle. "Do you like it? It's the new thing in riflery. It can shoot six shots one right after another and it only takes a few seconds to reload."

"Is it good at a distance?" Victor asked.

"Yes" Barnaby replied.

"Good I want you outside so you can handle any newcomers to the saloon." Victor said.

"Wait a minute Victor I am in this too! You're leaving me outside." Barnaby protested.

"Just for a minute to cover my back. You will have a vantage point from out there. She is here Barnaby. Contesa is here."

As Victor said this he thought of Jewels, Jose' and his father. It was so long ago but it all felt as it had happened yesterday. Then a hot flash of emotion hit him. It was the memory of Kendra, his only true light in centuries. For a moment he could hardly move with the grief of her death. How it was possible to love someone so much in such a short period of time, he did not know. But that is how it had been for them. Those were the cards dealt to him, and he to keep moving for now, so he pushed his emotions back.

CHAPTER TWELVE

VICTOR AND BARNABY RODE TO just down the street from the saloon and threw the reins over the hitching post. Not tied just laid over.

Barnaby took up a protected position across the street looking into the saloon. He could see most of the traffic going and coming from it, as well as a good view through the large windows. Victor sensed the vamps flickering past them slow up to smell them. Groups where flying overhead spying for dinner.

As he entered the crowded saloon the lights brightened and the noise dropped off. Immediately he counted eight humans and nineteen vamps. The saloon was filled with tobacco smoke, the smell of stale beer, and a hint of death... like a dead body. The saloon was painted green and red, the bar was maybe fifteen feet long with seven or eight tables which were mostly full of patrons. A set of stairs led up to a second floor merging with a hallway, which probably led to rooms that were rented for feasting. Victor sensed more vamps were up there. He was not worried. Soon they would be down where he was. Victor crossed the room toward the bar. About half way there he heard a familiar voice.

"Jane! It has been a long time Victor." It called from the second floor. It was Contesa Cortez. "You have come far to be with me Victor. Still riding the big black stallion Victor?" She said with an inquisitive but ominous tone in her voice.

"Have you figured it out yet Victor? I mean, about the stallion." She waited a moment. "You haven't! You've had over three centuries and you still don't know!" As she laughed the room went silent. "We wanted to feed on the purest blood of the Lipenstein. The rarest of all pure breeds. You still don't know Victor?" She moved across the landing like she was floating. "It's what separates us from the mindless ones. It's our savior." Contesa said.

"So you can rain down death and terror on mankind and feast on humans?!" Victor retorted.

"No, Victor. It is the cure for us. There are only a few breeds that are pure. The Arabian, the Lipenstein, the Welsh. But they are all contaminated now. Your colt we thought was our last chance, but we were wrong. There have been others like you Victor, and like your young friend outside. Not mindless, but with purpose. Now you know. Too bad you learned this too late!"

Contesa's face contorted, her arms became wings attached to her body, and her screech was deafening. Victor's eyes widened, his nose sank into his face, and large sharp fangs appeared. Victor turned and dropped to the floor. As he spun his sword sliced two vamps and a human that were near. Some of the humans ran for the door as the vamps were racing toward Victor. He jumped and spun again on his way up to the landing. Three more vamps turned to ash and dust. The ash would rise a few feet, then fall to the floor.

The glass in front of the saloon was shattered to shards from the rain of bullets from Barnaby's rifle. Humans and vamps were dropping like rain. Two more vamps were on the landing. Victor simply thrust his sword into the larger of the two and sliced upward while pulling his right pistol.

A blow from Contesa to Victor's left arm almost severed it completely. The sword of Spanish silver fell to the floor. Victor's arm swung down toward the floor in an odd direction. With his uninjured hand he shot once and a nearby smaller vamp's dust was floating down.

Suddenly Contesa was atop Victor. A shot from Barnaby's Henry caught her in the upper torso flinging her back. More vamps were coming down the hall. Victor unloaded his pistol blindly as he hit the floor. He was losing a lot of blood. He rolled, and as he did his right hand reached for the pistol on his left hip. He whirled his head around to get a shot off at Contesa. She was moving fast across the floor by the bar. One shot, two shots and she had disappeared. Victor blacked out, came to and then blacked out again.

When he awoke it was daylight but he was not in the saloon. He was not sure where he was. "It's a good thing you are a vampire Victor", Barnaby said smiling as if there was humor in this, "Sewing is not my thing friend. But there is not much of scar today. How does it feel?"

Victor held the bandaged arm up. "It seems to work. Although it hurts like hell."

"I'll bet." Barnaby said. "She almost sliced it off with her claws. Luckily my shot threw her off of you. And you were right. They came from everywhere inside and out. There must have been fifty of them from around the building, out of the sky, through the window. I thought I was going to melt the barrel of the rifle."

What about the humans? Victor asked.

"Some went for the door, some went for their guns, none of them made it out." Barnaby said.

"Where are we?" Victor asked.

"Outside of town, in the tent." Barnaby continued, "Contesa made it out Victor. I hit her with the one shot, but when she came out of the saloon I was in the middle of reloading and she was gone instantly."

Victor sat up. "We have to go after her." He groaned.

His arm hurt terribly and his head was swimming.

Barnaby said, "You must lay back down Victor. You've lost a lot of blood. You need to rest and eat." Victor knew he was right. "Here is fresh beef. Eat Victor." Barnaby handed him a large raw steak, dripping with blood. "You must regain some of your strength."

"Where are the horses Barnaby?" Victor asked.

"They're outside Victor. They're fine. Contesa said something about being cured because of pure lineage?" Barnaby asked. But Victor could not answer because he himself was unsure what her strange monolog had actually meant. Or was it just one of her tricks?

Maybe the horses had some type of antibody in them that could restore more of the human in us? Victor pondered. This would have to be researched. The University of Georgia Agriculture Department was known for its animal breeding program so it seemed like a good place to start. But first there were more vampires to be killed.

By nightfall Victor was ready to travel. The pair headed northwest toward Atlanta. The swarm of vampires had left its trail behind and it was not very hard to follow. Besides Miguel, Contesa, and Barnaby, Victor had only known the mindless vampires. If and when they stopped it was not to talk but mainly they would just stand there oddly. But make no mistake. They were fast and could leap a great distance. Ferocious eaters, one or two bites of their fangs and their victims could be headless. Victor had hoped they were going in the right direction to catch up with Contesa. It was time to settle the score with her.

As they rode through the night Victor thought more and more of Kendra and how things might have been. How the bullet should have taken his life and not hers. He thought of how her warmth from within had made him feel alive after all these years. Maybe someday, someway he would be with her. At that he closed his eyes to remember her magical inner beauty.

A week had passed and Barnaby and Victor were just north of Macon. The Civil War was starting. Human brothers and sons were going to start killing one other soon. But Victor could have never conceived how many of them were going to die. For the next six years blood stained the ground. The vamps feasted and feasted on the battles, especially at night. Thousands upon thousands of humans died and at the end there were thousands more vampires. Victor and Barnaby killed as many as they could. A lot of vamps were killed in battle themselves. Some were killed overhead. Some were killed feasting at night after the battles as countless humans lay dying. Sometimes all but a few soldiers would be dead and the vamps would kill them.

It was like a domino effect. One soldier was wounded then infected by a vamp. Then there were two to kill. The vamps were easy to kill and they had no sense of Victor or Barnaby. It was like shooting fish in a barrel; granted a lot of fish but nevertheless, fish.

As time passed which was quick for the two of them, it hardened them in a way unforeseen. Victor or Barnaby rarely talked but worked together intuitively as if by some unseen communication. It was just one battleground after another. More deaths and more senseless killing. Many times the humans were worse than the vamps as brother fought against brother to the death. For this period in time humanity was absent from their human vampire hearts.

CHAPTER THIRTEEN

THE WAR BETWEEN THE NORTH and the South was over now, and the vamps were getting harder to find. Barnaby had been a good companion and a true brother against the vampires, but he grew weary of the fight and secretly longed to return to his home in South Carolina. Adams Run was not far from Fort Sumter were they had been killing vamps.

After one particularly vicious battle, seeming out of nowhere Barnaby announced, "Victor, I tire of this killing." He was no longer smiling. "Adams Run, if it is still standing, needs me to look after it."

Victor agreed. A week later they arrived at the old plantation. It had survived, but the slaves were gone. "Guess I'll have to hire someone to help now, thanks to Mr. Lincoln." Barnaby said. They both wanted to smile but did not.

Victor rode Nightfire to the gravesite and dismounted. Barnaby followed kneeled down and put his hand on the head stone. "I am home sis!" Barnaby exclaimed quietly. Then got up and went to the house.

Victor stood there over her grave. "I love you. I still think of you as the light of my soul. There is still work to be done here. I hope to see you again."

Victor stayed on for a few days. Then told Barnaby, "I must go now. Contesa is still out there and others like her. They must die Barnaby." With that they shook hands. "Goodbye old friend."

He pointed Nightfire west where at least there was a promise of freedom. There were also tales of riches. Somewhere Contesa would feed her lust for human blood. As he rode westward, there was very little vampire activity.

He wondered if maybe Contesa was dead or perhaps in a different direction than the one he was headed. There was even the possibility of her living in a different country altogether. It really didn't make a whole lot of difference. He was going to try blending in. Going back to being a horse man didn't sound all that bad. Victor considered raising some real live horses and maybe some cattle. After all he did have to eat still.

As he rode west he hit a small pocket of vamps. Like hoof prints in the dirt he followed them to the next swarm. It was apparent someone or something was breeding vamps, but that vampire was smart and kept on moving. Victor was sure it was Contesa.

The trail reached Kansas City, traveled down to Texas, back to Oklahoma, then to Arizona. It was there were Victor ran into a bad bunch of humans and vamps. They had been riding roughshod over the townspeople. It was a quiet little place called Flagstaff; mostly farms and some cattle ranches.

It was dusk when Victor rode through town to a little livery stable. An older woman came out and said "Feed and water for you? That'll be a dollar and then twenty five cents a day."

Victor flipped her the dollar piece and said "Watch him he will bite." Victor would be back later with some chicken blood for his oats.

An old familiar sense was beginning to rise under Victor's skin. Vamps! He dusted off his long riding coat. Underneath was his sword and pistols. Light music and laughter was coming from the saloon; as always, a tavern. This or a place like it was where Victor had killed a thousand vampires in over three centuries. How funny that in one moment they were having the time of their life and the next, dead, ash and dust. A happy gathering before they were to go to meet their makers.

Victor entered through the swinging doors. Three vamps five humans. Four of the five humans were sitting at a card table. The barkeep was human. Two vamps each at one end of the bar. One female vamp sitting at a piano playing and singing Camptown Ladies. That one Victor wanted alive. She played piano, and most of all, she was not just a mindless bottom feeder. He walked slowly toward the middle of the bar.

"Whiskey coming right up." The bartender said. He brought the bottle and what looked to be a clean glass. "That'll be a dollar mister."

Victor put down his dollar on the bar.

"Where ya come from? East?" The barkeep asked.

"How long has she played piano for you?" Asked Victor, ignoring the question.

"Oh Molly? About three months. Pretty good ain't she?"

"Yup, for a vampire she's pretty good." Swiftly Victor pulled his pistols left and right. One shot from each and the vamps at each end of the bar went up in ash and then down in dust. Mollie the vampire took one step and then leaped at Victor. He side stepped her leap, grabbed her arm, and using her momentum he flung her into the wall hard. The throw would have killed a human but Molly the vampire was just dazed.

Victor grabbed her again, and out of the corner of his eye he caught sight of one cowboy rising and going for his gun. It was slow motion to Victor. His own gun aimed at the cowboys face before he could clear leather. The cowboy sat back down.

Molly was coming out of her daze, and changing back to her human form. As she did Victor grabbed her, rolled her on her belly and locked her arms between her shoulders pinning her there.

The bartender yelled, "What the hell is that? What's going on mister?"

"Get me some rope." Victor ordered.

"Here is some leather straps I use to hold the beer barrels down with. What did you do to the two on the end of the bar?"

Victor wasn't used to having to explain himself because usually everybody was dead.

One cowboy, the older one asked, "What's wrong with her?"

Victor said "She is infected with a disease. It's kind of like rabies."

They all stood up and backed off.

The bartender said, "Them others didn't look like rabies! That looked like black magic!"

"Well that's kind of what it was", Victor said, "but one thing for sure you would have been next. They weren't saying much were they?"

"Why no. And they been here a couple of nights."

Victor said, "You were lucky I came along. All of you."

"How did you know?" One of the cowboys asked.

"I seen it in the war back east." Explained Victor, "They get it. Then they want to give it to you. And they got to bite you to do it."

"What about Molly?" One asked.

"I will take her to my camp. I might be able to save her." And with that Victor picked her up and carried her out the swinging doors and a short distance from town.

She tried to bite, kick, and hiss at him. 'No good vamps.' Victor thought. He threw her hard on the ground, which took some of the fight out of her.

"You're not brainless. Quit fighting me!" he said. She didn't have much control of herself, so that meant she hadn't been a vampire for very long. Victor needed information.

"I want to know who turned you." Victor asked, as he tied her to a tree in a clearing.

She hissed a reply. "My mistress will kill you!"

"Ahh. Contesa. How long ago was she here?"

"Ain't telling you nothing cowboy vampire! My mistress is going to *kill you*!" She said again but this time she sang it.

Victor said, "You know the sun is coming up in a few hours. Tell me what I want to know and I will make it quick. If not you' ll burn and we both know what that's like."

It was about ten minutes before the sun was to come up. "Okay cowboy," said Molly who sounded more sensible. "She left a month ago. I wanted to go with her but she needs me to stay and feast on human blood. Not to kill them all, but to feast on them and then they would be mindless too and infect the towns people."

"A month you say. Which way was she going?" Victor asked.

"I don't know. She said she would back for me."

That was it. Contesa would start to turn a human and then leave it to infect more humans and create vamps to throw Victor off her trail and build her army. Smart he thought, very smart.

"That sun is coming up pretty fast, mister!" Molly sounded urgent.

"Yep, it sure is." Victor said looking around. "And you did pretty good." And with one stroke he sliced her head off. Ash and dust. Victor covered his face and eyes with his hat and mask and made his way back to the livery.

He got Nightfire and headed north about an hour until he came upon a little ranch house. Some horses were in the corral. Ten of them, Victor counted.

As he passed by, an old man came out and yelled, "Hey young feller!"

Victor halted Nightfire.

"You're the one that saved my hide last night! Come inside for some breakfast."

"No thanks, I got to keep moving" Victor said.

"Well, I didn't get a chance to thank you for what you did for me and some of the boys," He said.

"No thanks needed."

"Well, where are you headed," he asked?

"North, maybe west."

"My name is Charlie McCoy." He held out his hand to Victor.

"Victor Jane", he said as he reached down and shook Charlie's hand.

"How's about we make a deal, Victor?"

"What kind of a deal?"

Charlie explained, "I've got some prime beef about a mile and a half from here, just over the hill there. Are you interested?"

"Why would you think that, Charlie?"

"Something you said last night, about the war. Thought you might be done with killing and maybe settle down somewhere."

It hit Victor like a bolt of lightning. The old man was right. It *was* time for Victor to try something new.

Victor said, "How much?"

"Oh, for you, ten dollars a head. Me and my boys will help ya cut them out of the herd."

Victor said, "Okay, I've got two hundred dollars."

"I will get my horse," Charlie said.

The two rode for a short distance.

"Well, there they are." Said Charlie.

There were about seven or eight hundred by Victor's count.

Charlie said, "I'm gettin' about twenty-five dollars a head from the Army."

Just then, two more cowboys rode up.

"Hey boys, this is Mr. Jane. This is Earl York and Clem Hatfield. Boys, cut Mr. Jane about thirty head out."

"Charlie, I told you I had about two hundred dollars."

"Yeah, I know, and you're going to get thirty cows for it. My way of thankin' you for last night."

Back at the cabin, Charlie wrote up a bill of sale. "If you want to stick around for a day or so, the boys will make up a brand." He said, handing the paper to Victor.

It was a T. They bent the end of it and made a lazy J out of it. Victor was taken back by the gesture.

"Well, thanks fellas. I don't rightly know what to say."

"Good", Charlie said, "Rustle us up some of those beef steaks. Clem, we've got some brandin' to do in the morning". And with that Victor was now a cattleman. Now, he just needed his own ranch.

CHAPTER FOURTEEN

VICTOR TRAVELLED NOW UP THROUGH the Prescott Valley, and on up to Page, Arizona, there was plenty of green grass up that way, and water. From there Victor turned the small herd West. Thirty head of cows was a lot for one man and one horse. But Victor was no regular man, after all. He was more vampire than human.

He had sensed no vamps all the way from Flagstaff, Arizona. 'Too isolated', Victor thought, 'not much in the way of humans out here.' The home and ranches tended to be far apart, fifty miles in some cases. The weather was turning a little cooler. That would be better for the cattle because of the long stretches through the desert that would be coming up soon enough.

Victor left his herd about a mile out of Saint George, and went in for some supplies. He was a little low on cartridges for his pistols. Victor also thought it was time for a cattleman trail outfit, maybe a tent and some pots and pans. Add to that a pack horse, and maybe some coffee. He had always liked the smell of coffee. Even though, there was no need for it. The only thing he needed was blood. If he had fresh blood to drink Victor was good to go.

But now Victor wanted to be a cattleman, so he was going to look and be one from the bottom up. Victor had built a pretty handsome fortune over the centuries. He had gotten rubies from Russia and jade from China, and traded over the years in real estate, business and homes. He owned castles and buildings all over Europe. Most had been acquired as homes if killing vampires was going to take a while in a certain area.

Victor had also invented things like hardware for guns and rifles. The Jane name held at least fifteen patents in the U.S. So, Victor always had money. Well, out here he had gold; about ten pounds of it. More than enough to buy whatever he wanted. And if it was more, he could just send a bank draft from one of his numbered accounts back in New York.

Victor secured his supplies and started moving the herd west. He wanted to get to California. There, he would turn northward toward Oregon. He had never been there before, but he had heard there was lots of green *grass*. Within a month, Victor was headed up the back side of the Sierra Nevadas in California. The cows were plenty rested. He didn't want to push them hard if he didn't have to. The herd was keeping about a eight to ten mile a day pace.

It was about dusk when the stranger rode up the trail toward Victor. "Howdy".

Victor stopped his small herd.

"My name is Dave Chipp. I ride out of Rancho Lucy."

"Yeah, where's that at?"

"Oh, just outside old man Baker's field, just north of here. Where ya headed?"

"Oregon. How far back is the trail?"

"Oh, about a days ride. Hard to miss it. What's your name, cowboy?" "My name is Victor. Victor Jane."

"Well Victor Jane, hope you find plenty of grass for your cows in Oregon. If not they say Montana is just about Cowboy Heaven."

The two rode off in their own respective directions.

-The Legacy Continues-

Book Two

CHAPTER ONE

ALONG THE INTERSTATES OF AMERICA, there are many things to see, hear, smell, touch and taste...Such as blood.

Victor Jane is a vampire who originally hailed from Avies, France. He was born in the early fifteen hundreds.

At the age of twenty five Victor was changed into a vampire by a blood lusting vampire named Contesa Cortez and her brother Miguel. They were attacking Victor's purebred horses, a mare and a colt from Lipenstine, Spain. The mixture of the two bloods from the vampires and the horses had turned Victor into a super-vampire...and a super vampire killer.

Contesa had killed his brother Jose' that same night Victor had become a vampire. And a few years later his sister Jewels was killed on their horse farm in Avies France. It had been particularly brutal.

Now Victor, over four hundred and fifty years later travelled the highways and byways of the world to find and prey on vamps, as he refers to them. Victor's motto is simply, "THEY ALL MUST DIE."

Over the years there had been thousands and tens of thousands of vampires. There had also been bad humans to kill. There were bad humans that hook up with vampires, for whatever the reason may be. For some it is eternal life. For some, the lust of the vamps to feast on blood or flesh. For others it is the seduction of the vampire. Whatever their motivation, they all must die too.

After all, humans are food. Victor tried to stay on a diet of beef blood, and raw steak. But we all know how hard it can be to stay on our diets...

Victor now lived on a "small" ranch outside Butte, Montana. The remoteness is why Victor had chosen it many years ago. There were very high mountains and vast pastures in the valleys below that were perfect for his livestock. Victor had been building his cattle herd for a little over one hundred and fifty years, as well as a herd of sheep.

But his purebred horses were really what Victor Jane lived for...as much as a vampire can live. He kept the numbers of animals at a low count so as not to be noticed. Most of the cattle were sold off. The sheep and horses were for research for the cure of the vampire infection.

The 70,000 acre ranch was called Kendra's Heights. For the light in Victors life had once been Kendra Collingsworth. She was killed almost two hundred years ago. She had thought that even though he was a vampire, Victor still had some part of him that was human. A humanity that could feel love and the warmth of another being...something besides death... and the lust of the feast. Still Victor held onto this lifeline if you will. A glimmer of shining hope for himself. Hope that somehow he wouldn't spend an eternity in hell without his beloved Kendra.

CHAPTER TWO

VICTOR HAD LIVED THROUGH THE industrial revolution and into modernism. He had been a pilot in WWI and a tank driver in WWII, still killing vamps along the way. Because where there was war, there were vamps.

The "flicker" type are mostly mindless vampires that just feed on blood and flesh, these vamps were never turned, just bitten and let loose. A favorite practice of one Contesa Cortez.

She was the mother of vampires herself, a festering blight on Earth. Wherever she went, mindless vamps flourished and multiplied.

Victor's sole purpose was to rid the world of vampires. As the world changed the methods of killing changed also. Victor created more sophisticated weapons and devices to track, hold and kill vamps. His first and most important piece of equipment was his custom built semi truck.

A 2000 Peterbuilt with its one thousand horse-powered engine was twin supercharged, dual fuel pumps, and custom computerized to force mega fuel mixture down the throat of his modern monster. It also had a five gallon nitrous oxide system that could rocket the big rig to over two hundred miles an hour in just a few short seconds, reaching the maximum thrust of the eighteen speed, overdrive transmission. The truck was equipped with blackout windows that could be controlled with a flick of a switch. The sleeper area was formed from two sleepers welded together and customized. To the normal eye it looked like home sweet home for any truck driver. A small kitchen, small bathroom, queen bed, flat screen TV, lots of storage, and fold down couches that also made into a table. But under each piece of furniture, behind every shelf, and in the floor, in every conceivable place Victor's weapons were stored. The truck was a virtual fortress. It had specially reinforced tires, bulletproof glass, and plated side armor. All this extra protection was heavy so Victor only carried a few head of cattle at a time.

There was also an ample supply of blood. It was a special formulation from his stock. It kept him more human than vampire. The trailer was just a common livestock trailer with a compartment for his horse Nightfire who sometimes accompanied him on runs.

Victor travelled mostly at night as did the vamps. Tonight Victor had the big rig heading south on I-15 through Idaho Falls, Idaho. The end destination was Las Vegas, Nevada.

Looking for Vamps wasn't as easy as it used to be. They were smarter now. They blended in better. They used money and power to do this. Usually they had bodyguards and high tech security systems, the best money could buy.

Victor had also gone high tech. He had developed a database of areas where humans were disappearing. He had infrared scopes to track heat changes in the air. To the untrained eye the trails looked like heated air. Victor wanted to tag and release, but you just cannot let the vamps feed on humans. So catch and kill was the only solution. But Victor's senses were still his best weapons.

Victor guided the big rig as it rumbled to a stop just outside of town at Big D's Truck Plaza. The parking lot was full as usual. More trucks, less parking. Nobody wanted the big smelly noisy rigs in their town. The fuel islands were empty. Victor secured a spot at the first pump, fueled, and washed the little windows. He checked his oil and coolant under the hood then walked around, checking his lights and tires. As he nearly always was he getting a feeling of vamps, a flicker here and a leap there.

A part of Victor's new arsenal was a signal disrupter. It sent out a ping of electromagnetic energy which would disrupt the vampire's motion or block their "radar" temporarily. Simply put, it could stop them in their tracks. If the vamps were in the air they would have to restart their flight patterns.

Victor moved on into Big D's. The scent of vampires was everywhere. But Victor only counted two inside and they were behind the fuel desk.

"Pump two please", he murmured.

The vamp smiled. "Receipt?"

"Yeah". Victor's silver Desert Eagle .45 blazed fire from the end striking the first vamp between the eyes. The second vamp leapt toward Victor. The second and third bullets flipped the vampire sideways like a circus cartwheel as they both turned to ash, then dust.

The night came alive with vampires and humans. The high pitched sounds of the vamps and crazed noise of the loyal humans were closing in on Victor fast. At least seven came from the restaurant, and five from the storage room in the back. It was always dangerous with vampires. One wrong move might be Victors last. When the interfering humans were added to the melee it made things interesting to say the least.

Victor pulled the trigger of the big gun and six balls of ash turned into dust. The shock from the gun shook the inside of the store like a small earthquake. 4 more shots and human blood covered the room in a fine spray. Two more vamps ran across the wall toward the door. Victor reached for his sword made of fine silver from Spain. The vamps turned and came for him. But at the last possible moment Victor slashed in a horizontal motion. The bodies of two were instantly cut in half then burst into fiery ash, then dust.

Victor thought about his Samurai instructor and thought how proud the old man would be. He moved back to the counter, retrieved his receipt, and slowly exited the truckstop. He could feel a large movement of vamps exiting also, maybe a band of thirty or so.

Back in the truck Victor turned on the radar and could see the swarm moving in a southwest pattern too fast for his truck. But he could still track them for a while. Victor pulled the big rig back on to Highway US 12 then turned onto Interstate 15 headed toward Salt Lake City.

CHAPTER THREE

THE BIG BLACK PETERBUILT TRUCK with its Double Eagle sleeper and chrome wheels looked to be just another big rig. But it was Victor's lair, his coffin, his laboratory.

When he would catch a vampire alive he could perform experiments on them such as blood work ups for the severity of infection, metabolism, changes in skin, hair, even the progression of fang or tooth lengths, or frequency of their vibration, which often propelled the vamps. And in conclusion Victor had determined that vampires were big, ugly bats that needed to be killed. So, capture? Yes. Release? No. They all must die.

There was not much going on along I-15 tonight. Rolling through Salt Lake City Victor checked his equipment. The radar only showed a plane or two. He had lost the swarm. He wished he had applied the disruptor at the truck stop. It may have brought down a few vamps. He would be sure to try it next time...and there *would* be a next time...there always was.

Victor steered his rig south through Provo to St. George, then followed the freeway as it turned more west toward Las Vegas. He pulled the big rig into a rest area just north of the city. It was half an hour until sunrise.

He wanted to feed and water his livestock, except for Nightfire his four hundred and fifty year old stallion. Nightfire still looked to be about four years old. Like Victor, the horse did not age. After he was finished and Nightfire was in this compartment on the truck, Victor climbed back into the cab of his big rig. He turned the APU on.

The Automatic Personal Unit came on the windows automatically darken then the inside light came on. In a moment the cab hummed with electronic gear. Two outside infrared cameras, radar, and hypersonic metabolic microphones could pick up sounds from over two thousand feet away and isolate it. But still, his instincts were his best chance to kill vamps.

Victor ran a system check on the trucks fluid levels, fuel, oil, water, and blood. He hadn't eaten for a couple of days so he had a large chalice of bovine blood and a large cut of raw steak, his second favorite thing to eat. Humans were his number one favorite, after all they were food. Victor was now ready to settle in for the night.

The computers would work today while he slept. They were good about recording activity within a mile around the truck. It showed patterns of high frequency movement. That meant if vampires were moving by truck, train, or plane, they could still be tracked by their vibrations or signal. The smart ones moved all of the time which made it hard to find them. One day in California, the next in Ohio, feeding at night on their victims. Most vamps travelled in patterns. By logging the patterns Victor had an educated guess where they might be showing up next and right now those patterns were saying Las Vegas. And Victor expected a very large swarm.

Little did Victor know, they weren't just going to swarm, they were nesting.

CHAPTER FOUR

NIGHT FELL AND VICTOR BEGAN gathering the day's information from the computers and high tech sensors located outside the big rig. As the sun dropped from the desert sky evening fell upon the truck. The windows day tint was shut off and again they were clear. All monitors were placed back into the hideaways in the walls of the truck.

Victor chose a pistol for himself from the door of the armory where he kept his favorite, the Desert Eagle. He pulled on his duster jacket which concealed his sword. He put on his bull hauler cowboy hat and stepped from the truck making his way to the compartment where Nightfire was kept. It always made Victor feel good to be with his lifelong companion. He walked the big stallion in a small exercise circle for a half hour then watered and fed the livestock. Then it was time to check the rig.

Victor started the one thousand horsepower engine and let it idle while it powered up the systems onboard. Oil pressure and turbo, water temperature, air pressure, etc. Victor checked tires with a light and made sure there were no leaks and everything was tight. Because at two hundred miles an hour you don't want things coming apart.

Back inside the cab Victor plotted his course for the day. All legal paper work was completed and all electronic log books were brought up to speed. Better safe than sorry officer. Victor stayed as legal as possible.

The computer showed a course of southeast through Las Vegas somewhere near Boulder Dam just outside of town. The big rig rolled through the town with all of the twisted neon lights blinking white and yellow. Victor thought, "This must be what it was like to travel through a galaxy in deep space.

Victor's senses started to pick up vamps so he ran a computer scan, radar and sonar. All of the energy was flowing in the same direction almost in a cone or funnel. The conversion spot was the dam or very close to it.

He rolled the big truck to a stop on the west side in a large dirt pull off made by trucks and RVs, busses and cars over the years. The computer showed that the main concentration of the swarm was somewhere down in the canyon below.

Victor armed himself with two automatic pistols with extra magazines. Each holding fifteen rounds, then ten more mags on his bandelero belt. His two colt peacemaker 45s in holsters and ten speed loaders made a complete circle around his belt. The duster could generate fifty thousand volts and a single slap from it could fry a vamp. Victor had built his vampire disrupter into his Longhorn belt buckle. One push of the eye of the bulls head could stop a vampire in its tracks. At least for a few moments. Victor also had some well placed daggers in his boots, and waist band of his trousers. He had developed a flash grenade with UV light that was very nearly sunlight. Popping off one UV grenade was like being at a barbeque, ala vamp. They were small so they could hang eight or so on the inside of his duster comfortably.

Victor moved from the cab of the rig to the trailer where Nightfire was kept. The big stallion had sensed the vamps also and was rearing to go. Victor saddled his friend for battle. Along with armor for his chest, was leather around his neck. A blood sucker would have a hard time getting through to the horses jugular vein. Victor had a 30-30 Winchester in the scabbard on the saddle. He mounted the Lipenstein stallion, hit the remote alarm, and security systems on the big rig which included a high pitch sounding alarm and 50,000 volts to the touch came to life.

CHAPTER FIVE

VICTOR SPURRED NIGHTFIRE DOWN THE trail into the canyon below. They descended in a zigzag pattern. Victor senses were ablaze. Overhead movement and flickers were passing him and his big horse, unaware whatsoever of Victor. They were too busy to get to the feast below. The overhead vampires dove down to the bottom of the canyon. As he neared the bottom he could see a man-made trail going into the canyon wall. About 200ft from the entrance was a concave area on the trail. Victor reigned up Nightfire, dismounted, and put the reins on the ground and placed a twenty pound rock on them. Victor did not want his friend to go after him into the tunnel. But the rock was not so heavy he could not pull away if he needed to. "I won't be long boy". Victor said aloud to his horse. He retrieved his Winchester rifle and started through the opening of the tunnel.

The tunnel was about fifteen feet high and about ten feed wide. Storage or perhaps access to the inner working of the dam itself, Victor thought to himself. Forty feet in it became dark. The floor was covered with dirt which seemed to absorb some of the droppings and urine from the vampires. They seemed very excited. "Pissing themselves", Victor thought aloud.

As he continued forward the tunnel opened into a small ten foot by ten foot room which appeared to be a checkpoint or receiving area. It all looked to be abandoned. Ahead a second room opened up. This room was about half the size of a football field. This room was half filled with vampires. They were everywhere. On the ceiling, the walls, crammed together on the floor. They seemed to be centered on some kind of large creature in the middle of the room.

As Victor moved closer a vampire stopped right in front of him, turned and looked him straight in the eyes then let out a howling screech! Before the vamps face stopped changing Victor got off six shots, including one under the chin of the howling vamp.

In seconds Victor had reloaded twice. Burning vampires were everywhere. A hundred shots, and ninety nine vampires went up in smoky ash then fell into dust. The magazines for the Desert Eagle were all gone. The barrels of the guns glowed dull red. Victor discarded them and pulled both Colt 45's. More ash, more dust. The speed loaders worked very well, but it does take a split second, which gave the vamps an opening. Two vampires lit on his back, clawing and biting.

He rolled, smashing the two into the concrete wall face first. Two reloads left and still nowhere near the center of the room! Victor was right of center. He wanted to be in the center. Even after all twelve shots thundered it gave him a little room but still not where he wanted to be. The Colts were empty. He holstered them out of habit.

As his hand came from his holster, he flipped two flash grenades on the right side of the big room. A loud explosion, then bright emanating like a sunlight burst caught the right side of the room on fire as one vamp after another burst into flames.

'Talk about your instant suntan!', Victor thought to himself smiling. And with that two more grenades went off, this time toward the left side and again the room lit up as sixty or more vamps were set on fire. The ash looked brilliant against the darkness then again fell to dust.

Victor tried to get to whatever it was in the center of the room but it was too late. At least seven vampires were already on him ripping his duster off, clawing and biting. Almost unconscious now, Victor was dragged across the room and dropped directly in front of the giant queen or king vampire. Which he could not tell.

What he could see was at least eight feet tall. It was a vampire face alright but it had four long arms with claws, sunken eyes, and no nose, just a hole where a nose should be. Some hair around its long pointy ears, its skin was very clammy looking like it was sweating. The body was set atop a large sack that sat on the ground probably six feet square. It was moving like boiling oil and was a dull yellow color.

Victor could not believe his eyes. The vamps were mounting the large creature from behind one after another, then switching every few seconds. Then Victor heard an old familiar voice.

"Victor! You looked so much better last time when we met!"

He managed to hiss back a return, "CONTESA!"

Contesa addressed the Queen Vamp. "This is Victor Jane, a pure blood Lipenstein. Only a few remain on this planet. And now my Queen, you have him! Enjoy your feast!"

At that moment Victor reached for his belt buckle disrupter. He hit the button and all vamps in close proximity were rendered helpless for a couple of seconds. This gave Victor the opportunity to move, and move he did! His sword lay between Contesa and the Queen Vamp. Victor rolled in between the two, grabbed his sword, and swung himself up on the back of the Queen. With two deadly strokes of the sword the bag was separated from the Queen and little vamp eggs went everywhere. As The Queens body fell, Victor rode her body forward onto the floor. Contesa leapt at Victor making a slash at him. He leaned back as far as possible but was still struck by the blow which made him flip backward. As he did the silver sword came up severing Contesas' right arm just below the shoulder. Victor fell to the floor.

Vampires were scrambling to get out of the big room. The orgy was over. Victor heard a loud racket by the door. It was Nightfire stomping vamps. They were on his back and neck and now under his hooves. The stallion was too much for them. He smashed, threw and stomped vampires into the ground. Victor grabbed the last stun grenade, pulled the pin from the shredded duster, and threw it into the large sack of vampire eggs. The explosion caused a chain reaction, and the eggs sounded like firecrackers going off rapidly.

Victor ran for the stallion, leapt to his back, then turned and spurred the big horse out of the tunnel, and up the trail to the truck. Daylight was breaking and Victor rushed to get Nightfire into the trailer. His own skin was starting to smoke.

He hit a secret button on the outside of the truck that opened its doors, then dove in and secured the doors. With that all systems came on. Blackout windows and security fortified the truck. Victor was burned, cut, bitten, scratched, and clawed very badly. It would take at least a few days to heal. In the meantime he needed to move the truck.

CHAPTER SIX

VICTOR LAY THERE OVER THE steering wheel. A loud knock came at the truck door. It couldn't be a vamp. They would burn right about now. Then another loud knock!

"Hey! Open up in there! I can help!" It was a woman's voice. "I saw you were hurt! Come on! Let me look at your wounds! I'm a nurse! If you don't open up I'll have to call the police!" There was something different about the voice. European he thought. And with that he opened the driver's door.

Victor was drained of strength as he tried to move toward the back of the truck sleeper. He didn't make it. Even a vampire will pass out from loss of blood. It seemed like he was in a dream. He and Nightfire were flowing along the sky. But he did not feel dead. But he never did. After all he was a vampire.

Victor awoke and saw a young woman sitting in the driver seat. "Who are you and where are we?" Victor said through the pain, most of which came from his neck.

"Oh, you must lay back down. You have lost a lot of blood. We are in Kingman, Arizona. My name is Sabrina Stalinsky. I am a nurse. I bandaged your wounds. I am very good but not that good. You seem to be healing. I cleaned and dressed the cuts. The bruising and bite marks I cleaned also."

"Would you care to explain how we got to Kingman," Victor asked groaning, "and what were you doing at the dam?"

"I grew up on a big farm with big tractors. My father has been letting me drive them since I was about five. I am on vacation from Warsaw, Poland. I was on the tour bus parked close to your truck. The tour was inside the dam. I forgot my camera and went back. That is when I saw you ride up to the truck. You're lucky I saw you were hurt. I also cleaned up your horse and put away his saddle and breast plate and neck guard. Now do YOU want to tell ME what the hell was going on at the dam?"

Victor thought for a moment then replied, "I'm a four hundred and sixty year old vampire seeking revenge on all other vampires. They all must die." He croaked.

Sabrina laughed heartily for a moment then stopped and asked, "No really. What happened back there?"

Victor did not say a thing, just looked at her.

"C'mon", said Sabrina, "Was it a motorcycle gang or maybe it was a rodeo? Is that it?"

Victor still did not say a thing, but for a brief moment allowed himself to change into a vampire. Sabrina froze with fright and could not speak or move.

Victor said, "Don't worry. I'm not going to eat you. I only eat bad humans, so relax Sabrina." He smiled. "Some vacation you're having. One you won't forget I am sure."

With that Sabrina spoke cautiously. "You don't look a day over twenty five years."

"Good guess", he replied, "and thank you for helping Nightfire and myself."

"So that is his name, Nightfire. I kept asking him but he would not say. Playing shy probably?"

Victor smiled again, "He does that around beautiful women."

"Why did you name him Nightfire?

"I didn't, my sister did. She raised him."

"How long for you to heal all the way...I am sorry. You know who I am. What is your name?"

"Victor Jane. And usually a couple of days most of the time."

"Do you do this a lot Victor? I mean, battle vampires and bad humans?"

"You talk a lot don't you?"

"Only when I am nervous. And right now I am sitting here talking to a four hundred and sixty year old vampire! A real live vampire!" A pause, "You are alive right?"

"As alive as a vampire can be. How about you? How long have you been a nurse?"

"You know Victor, I know maybe a hundred nurses," she stopped, "Five years. And you should rest now."

CHAPTER SEVEN

AFTER TWO DAYS VICTOR WAS back at full strength and not a mark on him. Sabrina was impressed. "It is nothing short of amazing, your healing capabilities. In my professional opinion most humans would have died from those wounds. The medical ramifications are staggering. I mean, learning your secret could save a lot of lives Victor."

Victor considered how smart she was which moved something inside him. She was five foot ten and had long black hair so shiny you could almost see yourself in it. She had deep blue eyes that reminded him of sapphires. When she smiled it lit up the room. Victor wanted her. It had been an hundred and fifty years since he had been in love with his beloved Kendra. Now the same feelings were beginning again, only this time for Sabrina.

She was cooking something in the galley.

"I hope you're hungry Victor. All you have is steak in here to eat."

"I like mine very raw", he replied. He had kept some food staples for appearances. Canned goods, a bottle of sherry, and two gallons of bovine blood in the refrigerator.

She set the table. "Come and eat Victor." She was happy with what she had cooked for dinner.

Victor closed the laptop he was working on. At least he was pretending to be working.

They sat at the table and Sabrina asked, "Is this your home Victor?"

"No", he said, "It's more like a home away from home. I have a small cattle ranch in Montana. How about you? Where do you live?"

"I live in London right on Hyde Park." She liked the small talk with Victor. It made her feel safe, as if she had known him a long time and she felt like she could say anything to him. Could it be she could feel herself attracted to him?

"Are you married Victor?"

"No. You?"

"No."

They both looked at each other a little too long then laughed aloud. Victor had not laughed for a very long time. They talked for hours of Warsaw; of Spain; her family; his family; of her work at the children's hospital of Manchester, England; of his ranch in Butte, Montana.

She wanted to kiss him. He stood over the sink washing the dishes. She watched him. Vampire or no, she wanted him. She moved close to him.

"Here. I will dry for you."

As she reached for the towel their hands touched and they turned and looked deeply into each others eyes. Victor grabbed her and kissed her very deeply. The embrace was held most of that evening and well into the night as they made love.

Sabrina was in ecstasy. A few seconds for her was an hour for Victor. Time to explore her innermost feelings and heighten her senses so extremely that she was in and out of consciousness throughout the night. To her sometimes, it felt as if they were floating on clouds over cities; heat like an oven on her body; pressure of a waterfall; heavy vibration from her inside out; the most pleasure she could feel without dying. The vibrations were to the point she would curl around him twisting her body as a survival mechanism from the rapid deep motion. At times it was hundreds of strokes per minute which brought her to orgasmic release of at unnatural rate.

Victor lost control changing from human to vampire and back again. As a human the emotions were deep and rhythmic. As a vampire they were lustful.

In the morning Victor awoke. It seemed as if it was the first time in centuries. Sabrina lay in his arms. She seemed fragile, even delicate.

Victor thought to himself, "I could...She could...No. I must let her go." To stay with him surely meant death. If not by the vamps, by him if he lost control and needed to feast on her blood. He did not know. He hadn't last night. But he had wanted to.

Victor slowly moved through the truck to the driver's compartment. He looked through the window to see if he recognized anything familiar sights. He didn't. They looked to be at a truck stop in the desert. Sabrina had said Kingman, Arizona. It was ten o'clock in the morning. The sun was hot and very bright. Victor checked the outside temperature; already ninety-six degrees. The barometric pressure was low. No clouds in sight. With the camera on, he checked the trailer outside and inside. Nightfire looked fine. He would look closer later this evening.

"How does it look? The parking I mean?" Sabrina said groggily from the back of the sleeper.

"It looks fine. Good job."

"I'm not afraid anymore," she said. "I don't know if I can do another night like last night though."

"I was thinking the same thing," he said without emotion, "I could have killed you."

"But you didn't. That has to count for something?"

"I'm sure it does Sabrina. But I cannot take that chance again with you. I did want to kill you last night for a moment. I wanted to feast from your blood!"

"Alright...what about turning me into a vampire?"

"No. You would hate me and what you would become. When your friends and family die, life begins to lose purpose or meaning. As a vampire you would kill for the lust of feasting on flesh and blood."

"Is that what you do Victor? Lust and feast on humans?"

"No Sabrina. Not as a rule." He felt tired. "But I do kill humans. Bad ones most of the time. I must rid the earth of vampires and the infection that they bring. So far I am the only one that can. They all must die."

"And does that include you Victor?"

Victor changed the subject. "We must move the rig. It's been here too long."

CHAPTER EIGHT

AFTER VICTOR HAD PERFORMED ROUTINE inspections he fired up the big rig and headed west. Interstate 40 was hot and desolate. After about an hour they were through Needles, California.

"Victor," Sabrina said, "isn't that a sleeping volcano?" She pointed at a large mountain out in the desert. Victor just nodded.

He had started getting beeps on his computer. The radar was picking up some vamps moving in the area.

"They must have some kind of vehicle," he thought, "a truck or a charter bus."

The computer was set for vibrations of vampire movement. Victor quickly slowed the big truck. The computer was only good for about a half to one mile. He pulled the truck to a stop alongside the road and plotted a course into the computer. In a matter of a few seconds a map popped up on the computer screen showing where the vampires were and which way they were traveling. It was two in the afternoon and the sun was high and hot. Victor used the long range camera to try and view where they were.

Yes! There it was! An old RV out on an old dirt road moving very slow so as not to raise much dust. The dirt road was skirting the highway.

Victor said, "We will follow them for now; see where they are going. Fuel was at half a tank which meant one hundred and fifty gallons. This made for eight hundred miles or so depending on how fast they were going and on what kind of terrain they were to cross.

They stayed back about a mile so as not to give away their advantage. They could follow with the cameras and sonar. Victor used the computer to follow aerially from a real time satellite. Thermal infrared imaging from the camera revealed two hot bodies; humans, and at least six vamps. The radar picked up on the vamps vibrations.

Victor pulled out one tenth on the satellite camera. It showed the dirt road leading toward an old mining camp or company. It was ten miles or so. He fed the coordinates into the computer and cross referenced state and county records with mining deeds. Bingo. There it was, The Lucky Clover Gold Mine. It had been closed down for seventy years. If Victor was right he would find more than gold there. There would be vampires... and lots of them.

By now Sabrina was sitting in the passenger seat. "What's our next move Victor?" she said eagerly, watching intently through the windshield.

"Our next move is to get you out of here. Back to Kingman or the bus stop in Needles," he said dryly.

"Wait a minute Victor. I am not going anywhere. Please. I can help."

"It's too dangerous", He said in a stern voice. "You saw what I looked like when you came to help me. I cannot take a chance on you getting hurt."

"Please Victor. I will stay with the truck. There may not be another chance like this for you to get those vampires. Maybe this RV is their ride out of here."

Victor thought for a moment. "Okay. But no matter what, you stay with the truck! If I don't come back in one hour you high-tail it out of here! You got that?!"

And with that, Sabrina agreed.

CHAPTER NINE

VICTOR PULLED THE BIG RIG onto the desert dirt road two miles from the Lucky Clover Gold Mine.

"This is where you will stay," he said to Sabrina. "A quick lesson in arms safety for you."

He pulled open the armory behind the driver side seat, and pulled out two 45 pistols with ammo belts. Next he pulled out two Mac 10 auto pistols with four long mags, as well as six grenades of the sunburst variety. Luckily he had made it out of the cave under the dam with his Colts and his sword. He loaded the holsters made for the quick loaders. Then he handed Sabrina a Smith & Wesson snub nosed 38 and a two shot 45 caliber derringer.

"They are loaded. Just aim and pull the trigger. Aim for their heads." Victor stopped. "Have you ever shot a gun?"

"Yes, my father and I used to hunt back in Warsaw."

"Ok, pistols are sighted the same as a rifle but at the end of your hand. The 38 has a safety lever here on the side," he pointed at it. "You have to release it," he said as he pushed it forward. "Now it is ready to fire. You must remember to release it. For the Derringer, just pull the hammer back then pull the trigger. Got it?"

"Yes I think so."

Victor unloaded the guns and showed her again how to aim and fire the weapons. A couple of dry fires then he reloaded them. "Remember. If I am not back in one hour, fire up the truck and go."

"Ok. I got it," Sabrina said.

It was now close to dusk. He showed Sabrina the monitor which showed vampire movement. "If this lights up red you've got about one minute to go. Whatever you do, do not stop. Once the truck is moving hit this big blue button. It activates security. OK?"

"OK", she said.

Victor readied himself for the night. He first strapped on his revolvers then the ammo belt for the 45 pistols and the Mack 10s. The two 45's went in the back in the Colts holster. The Mac 10s hung under his armpits with adjustable straps which allowed them to hang down for access at arm's length. He fastened the grenades to the inside of his new black duster. Then last he pulled on his black "big stumpy" hat and stepped out of the big rig, closing the door behind him.

Sabrina rolled the window down. "Are you taking Nightfire?"

"He would be pretty mad at me if I didn't," Victor replied.

With that Victor rigged up his big friend's saddle, chest plate, and neck armor while Nightfire munched on a handful of oats mixed with bovine blood. The big Lipenstein did not need it. It was more of a treat.

It was dark now. Victor went to the cab one more time. Sabrina rolled the window down.

"Watch the monitor. You can see most of what is going on. If you spot vamps, get the hell out."

As he turned Sabrina started to say something...but she didn't. Her eyes said it all. And Victor spurred the black stallion into the night.

CHAPTER TEN

THE LUCKY CLOVER GOLD MINE was a pretty good strike back in 1870. Wagon after wagon of gold ore had come out of it. In 1882 it was considered played out. 1940 it was reopened. According to records it had one main shaft about a half mile straight down with several smaller shafts at different levels. In 1949 it was closed again due to a cave-in which trapped three miners below. The mine was left closed in memorial to the lost miners.

Victor rode Nightfire to a small rise just before the mine. He could see down to the mines opening. It looked as if there was a long covered entrance into the shaft. There were two big RVs sitting by the mine. One was at the end of the covered walkway leading into the mine. Victor could sense three humans but no vamps.

"They must be inside", he thought to himself. Victor dismounted for a closer look. He wrapped the reigns around a small twig. That was to give the big horse a fighting chance if he was attacked by vamps. Three humans were together by the front of the RV closer to the mine. They were talking in low tones as if not to be heard but sound carries a long way in the desert. A small amber light was visible from the cigarettes. The smell filled the air as did the sound.

In one swift move Victor was standing in the middle of the three. The look of surprise only lasted a moment as two of their heads fell to the ground. Victors sword was at the third mans throat with just enough pressure so he could not scream out.

"How many vamps are down in the mine?" Victor demanded, then added, "You lie, you die."

The man was in his early twenties. He spoke very quietly. "Maybe fifty or so. But I am just a driver!"

With that Victor drove the sword up through his skull and out the back. He wiped the blood from the blade on his tongue and said, "Not just a driver. A *vampire* driver! You lied, you died!"

As he started down into the mine he heard a sound coming from below. A faint scream and the smell of bat guano burning. The mine had a gradual slope downward. The tunnel diameter was about ten feet with wooden support beams placed regularly. A small set of rail tracks were in the center of the floor. Victor could sense a lot of vibration coming from down below... and more screams.

Victor had gone about 600 feet when he came to a cluster of vamps on the roof, one on top of the other. They were getting ready to feast. Whatever was in the mine was dinner. The vamps crawled and scurried like cockroaches. Victors best chance was to go by so quickly that they would not notice. He flickered fifty yards past them to a smaller shaft opening.

Only one had looked up with his bat-like face and moved toward the opening where Victor stood inside. The creature crawled across the ceiling and poked his head into the opening of the smaller shaft. Its head rolled a few feet into the shaft, and the body remained stuck to the wall. Nobody noticed.

The deeper Victor went into the mine the louder the screaming became. Some were screams of pain. Some were screams of lustful pleasure. A feast!

Victor appeared at the entrance of a large room. Maybe one hundred feet square with air shafts leading to the surface. Victor could see only by the smoke of the lanterns rising, escaping through the ducts to the surface. Six humans were tied to timbers throughout the room. "Too late for them", Victor thought. Not bad humans, just dead humans.

Forty to fifty vamps were feasting and lusting in the blood and flesh. There were also vampires, smart ones who were just watching. He could tell they were loving it. Then Victor stood in the light for all to see... and they did see. Vamps started at Victor from all directions. One of the smart ones held out his hand and yelled for the others to stop, and they did. They froze in their tracks.

The big one spoke again. "Well if it isn't the vampire cowboy turned trucker! We are honored!"

"No you are DEAD!" Victor yelled.

"Oh please. Mr. Vampire killer, there are at least forty of us. Do you think you will get all of us?"

"Yes! That's my plan! Not that it matters, but who are you?"

"My name is Escabar Cortez Vega. Yes. I thought you might recognize the accent."

"You must be Contesas' brother?"

"Cousin, not too distant."

The other two smart ones were whispering to Escabar, "Pure blood of Lipenstein Spain. Is your horse nearby Victor Jane pureblood?"

"Close enough to smell you burning *vampire!*" He said as he tossed two sunlight grenades, one to the left side of the room, the other on the right side of the room.

The grenades had two second fuses but vamps move pretty far in two seconds. The vampires were coming at Victor from every direction but he had already lowered the Mac10s and opened fire. The Macs handled thirty round clips. It only took two seconds to empty both guns. By now there were vamps going up in ash from the flash grenades. Victor turned, disconnected the Macs and they dropped to the floor.

But before the guns hit the ground he released two more grenades at the entrance to the big room. These were fragmentation grenades with three second fuses. But Victor was forty feet up the mine shaft when they exploded sealing the vamps inside their tomb forever under several feet of dirt, broken timbers and rocks...BIG rocks. All were jammed tightly in the shaft. Smoke and dust billowed out of the mine. Victor rolled with the concussion of the blast into a kneeling position, his two 45's drawn from the back of his belt, each pointed in the direction of the mine.

Vamps were coming at him from both directions. He fired both pistols into the smoke and dust which began to light up like fireflies in fog. The vamps started to flee the mine. The smoke and dust was too much. Victor made his way out as he was emptying the 45's into random vamps.

Only three made it out. He pushed the empty guns back into the belt and pulled his colts from the holsters. He fired the left one and hit vamp number one in the back of the skull. He fired the right Colt and caught number two in the temple. They both turned to ash before falling to the ground in a pile of dust. Vamp number three was pretty far away. Victor shot both Colts until he saw the ash flame of the last vampire. Then he made his way up on the rise where Nightfire was waiting.

"Ok boy. Let's go."

As Victor rode by the air vent to the mine he could see black smoke coming from under the ground. "A good night's work", he thought. And he let Nightfire lead them back to the big rig.

CHAPTER ELEVEN

VICTOR RODE TO THE TRUCK. Something wasn't right. The big rigs doors were open. Victor reigned up Nightfire beside the rig. There had been a struggle and there were piles of dust from vamps about the truck, apparently electrocuted from alarm system. Several more were at the cab door. Why had she opened it? With a sinking feeling in his gut Victor thought, "I shouldn't have left her alone. I should not have even brought her with me."

Victor got to the monitors to track the vamps if he could. There they were a half mile out. At least he hoped that was them. Victor hurried Nightfire aboard the rig. The vampires were moving very fast across rough terrain. It had to be some kind of motorized vehicle, maybe a dune buggy. But Victor could not be sure. He pulled up the coordinates on the computer satellite. It took only seconds and there they were. They were headed west for the road. And with that Victor swung the Peterbuild westward on the asphalt.

He brought the rig up to speed and got a lock on the vamps. The tracking would be easy now. He hoped it wasn't too late and Sabrina was still alive. Victor roared the big rig into high gear. He was closing in fast. The speedometer was showing 185 mph. The outside looked like a blur. It wasn't a dune buggy. It was a Hummer H-2; a big and powerful SUV. But not as big as the Peterbuilt, nor as powerful.

As Victor closed in the back window opened and multiple weapons began firing on the truck. Victor could not take the chance on returning fire. Sabrina may still be alive. The only thing Victor could do was ram the Hummer and hope to spin it out of control. His truck was taking a lot of fire. It was built with bullet proof glass and reinforced steel panels. But even *it* had its limits.

The first tap from the Peterbuilt sent the Hummer out of control but it did not stop it. The next bump sent it spinning out into the desert. It took another three hundred yards to stop the big truck.

Victor hadn't reloaded his pistols yet. As he leapt from the truck he grabbed two quick loaders for his six shooters. He walked toward the SUV with purpose as he loaded the Colts. Fifty yards away the doors flew open, guns blazing and two humans jumped out. Bullets whizzed by Victors head as he fanned one of the Colts. Six shots, one second, two dead humans.

Sabrina exited the Hummer. Right behind her was Escabar holding what looked like a .44 magnum.

Victor spoke first. "I didn't think I would see you again Escabar."

"Yes Victor. I am very fast. I should have killed you when I passed you in the mine. Don't move Victor. I will kill your human plaything."

"You mean dinner don't you?"

Escabar had a moment of clarity and that was all Victor needed. He shot from the hip one shot between the eyes. Escabar fell back in an ashy plume then to dust.

Sabrina, crying and terrified, ran to Victors arms. "Oh Victor! I was so scared! I thought I was dead!"

"Exactly whose human are you?" he responded coldly. "Escabar's?"

"WHAT?! She screamed back at him in anger, "YOU THINK I BELONG TO ANOTHER VAMPIRE?! DO YOU THINK CONTESA OR ESCABAR PUT ME UP TO... WHAT VICTOR?! SPYING ON YOU, THE GREAT VAMPIRE KILLER TO GAIN YOUR CONFIDENCE?! WHAT VICTOR?! YOU TELL ME?!"

Victor said nothing. Then slowly, "It's Nightfire that you wanted. He is the only cure."

In a quick move he sliced off Sabrina's head. As it hit the ground he said, "Who ever said anything about Contesa?"

He could not feed on her. He had been taken in by her. Four hundred and sixty years had proven that he was not immune to his human side. She had left the truck on her own. They had sacrificed the vamps to try and fool him. Victor felt sick. It was an odd feeling for a vampire.

CHAPTER TWELVE

THE BIG RIG ROLLED INTO Barstow, California. There wasn't much going on in Barstow except a twenty acre salvage yard. Mostly semi-trucks from the desert highways. Victor pulled the truck around the side. He needed parts. The truck had been shot up pretty badly, and the big cattle bumper was bent. It was a few hours before daylight. He would feed and water the livestock. It would be a long day in and out of the sun for Victor. But as long as he stayed covered up he would be fine.

The salvage yard was run by and old man and his wife. He was a tall skinny fellow and she was as opposite as could be. The yard opened at eight a.m. and Victor went in.

"Billy's my name. This is my wife Jojo. She's just making some coffee. Would you like some?"

"No thanks", Victor said, "I just need some parts for my big rig."

"Well you come to the right place. Jojo and I been pulling cars, truck, vans, motor homes, trailer-houses, boats, you name it from off the road around fifty years. What is it you need?"

"Some lights. Mostly some cosmetic repairs."

"What year is your truck?"

"2000 Peterbuilt 378."

"You're in luck. We have three or four out in back. Hang on, I'll look it up on the computer. Yep. I got three Pete's 2000 model 378. Tell ya what! When his computer works it sure makes life a little easier." Billy chuckled and continued. "In the old days we would have had to walk out there and check. Anyway, its pick and pull. You bring the parts by here and pay as you go. Okay?"

"That's fine," said Victor.

Billy continued, "Anything big you need help with, let me know. Oh! You watch out for rattle snakes. This is the desert! Them snakes like the shade."

"Okay. I'll watch for them."

Victor went to the truck for his tool box and made a mental list of parts he needed. He worked on it the rest of the day. He straightened the cattle bumper. A new shroud for the radiator, and a new headlight and bracket. It was getting late in the afternoon and Victor was just finishing patching some bullet holes when Billy showed up.

"My wife cooked up beef stew in the crock pot. You're welcome to eat if you want."

"No. But thank you." he answered. "How much do I owe you?"

"Well let's see. Radiator, not cheap; Shroud, that's expensive too; Headlight and bracket; lets go with four hundred dollars. That sound fair to you?"

"That'll do," Victor said.

Billy went on. "You don't remember me do you Victor Jane? Or should I say, Captain Victor Jane, helicopter pilot, Korean Conflict medevac? You saved my life. I was wounded and left for dead. I will never forget what I saw and what you done for me. It is you isn't it Captain Jane? I don't know how it is possible!

"Demons from hell were there that day. Everything was moving in slow motion...'cept the demons, and you of course. I could see them eating the soldiers around me. Then I saw your chopper blades go overhead. Then a demon was just about to bite my head off when you showed up and blew *his* head right off! I remember thinking, 'That'll teach you demon!'

"Then you picked me up and put me on your chopper and flew me to a MASH hospital. I was almost a week unconscious. When I came to I was going on about the demons I saw...And the cowboy demon killer!

"I never got to thank you Captain Jane. They told me who you were at the MASH unit. I never forgot your face. The parts are on me. Free. No charge."

And with that he turned and walked away before his emotions could overtake him.

He had only gone a few steps when Victor said softly, "You're welcome Private Billy Casper."

Billy turned and smiled then kept walking.

Victor washed up, fired up the big rig, and headed west.

CHAPTER THIRTEEN

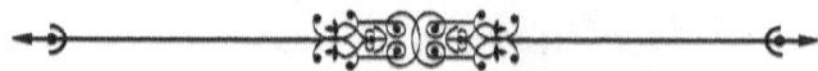

L.A. WAS THE STOP ON the way home to see an old, old friend, Barnaby Collinsworth. Victor hadn't seen Barnaby in a century. More like a century and a half! Victor had seen Barnaby on TV in the early 70's. It was some late night horror show and if Victor recalled correctly, Barnaby had been the host.

Barnaby had been the brother of Victors one true love, Kendra Collingsworth. Barnaby and Victor had waged war on the vampires who ultimately had been the cause of her death. Victor missed his old friend. The last few days events had Victor feeling his human side; an emotion he did not consider safe.

As he drove on he wondered why he had not killed Barnaby. After all, he was a vampire. Victor had always intended to kill him from the very beginning.

The register at the Hollywood Hotel is where Victor would find Barnaby Collingsworth, the actor. At least that is what his Facebook page said. A great thing Facebook. You could find most anyone in seconds if you know what to look for.

The big rig rolled down I-15 to I-210 to the I-5 Beverly Hills exit. A few more turns and Victor was parked in front of the Hollywood Hotel, a swank nineteen forties hotel rich in history with Hollywood's elite. Victor shut down the big rig, armed it, and went inside.

As he walked to the front desk, he had an overwhelming feeling of vampires around him. He was unsure where, but nevertheless, he felt them.

Victor rang the bell.

"Yes sir? May I help you?" the clerk asked in a chipper, energetic tone.

"Yes. I am here to see Mr. Barnaby Collingsworth. He is expecting me. My name is Victor Jane."

"Just a minute Mr. Jane. I will check for you."

The clerk rang a number. "Mr. Jane to see Mr. Collingsworth. Yes sir. Mr. Jane, Mr. Collingsworth is expecting you."

The clerk rang a bellhop. "Take Mr. Jane to the penthouse please." "Right this way sir." Said the bellhop as he led the way to the elevators. On the ride up the young bellhop said, "That Mr. Collingsworth. He sure is a good egg".

"Egg?" Victor asked.

"Oh I just meant he's a good guy. Everybody likes him."

The elevator opened to a hallway with one door. They stepped out and up to the door. The bellhop knocked lightly and a man in a butler suit answered.

"Right this way Mr. Jane."

Victor turned to the bellhop, "What's your name?"

"Frankie sir."

"Alright Frankie. Here's a twenty. Keep an eye on my truck out front?" "I will sir", he said as he turned and walked to the elevator.

Victor went into the apartment, if you could call it that. It was more like a palace in the sky. Barnaby came into the room. "Ah Victor! My oldest friend!"

Victor responded feeling much emotion, "Barnaby! How I have missed you old friend!", and the two embraced heartily.

"It is so good to see you Victor! Robert, Chivas please."

"Yes sir, right away." Replied the butler.

"Victor, please come into the living room and sit."

"Nice place Barnaby."

"Just somewhere to hang my hat. What about you Victor? Where is home?"

"Montana. I have a little place just outside Butte."

"Still cowboy-ing I see." Barnaby said looking at Victors attire.

"That and truck driving."

"Truck driving?! With all your power and money?"

"It's a very nice truck."

"Oh I am sure of that. It is sure good to see you Victor. Do you still have Nightfire?"

"Yep. I keep leaving the barn door open but he won't go!"

They both laughed aloud.

Robert, the butler returned with the drinks.

"Victor, I think about her every day. I still miss her terribly."

"So do I Barnaby. She is still the only one for me."

"She loved you with her heart and soul Victor. Ah Cheri." Then he stood and raised his glass. "TO KENDRA! OUR UNIVERSAL LIGHT!"

"To Kendra," Victor repeated reverently, saluting with his glass.

"So Victor, what brings you here after all these years? To kill me maybe?"

"No Barnaby. Not to kill you."

"What were your famous words? 'They all must die!' I always considered that also meant you and I Victor."

"It does Barnaby. I just hope you and I will be the last to go."

"You haven't found her yet, the Contessa?"

"Yes, I have found her several times. She always escapes. She set quite an elaborate trap last time. Barnaby, I sensed vamps when I first arrived."

"Yes Victor, they are in and out of here all the time. Actors want to live forever so they pal up with them. Actors love to be seduced by them. As you know, there are some vampire actors. You see, the thing with acting is that you can only do it a short time or the industry sees you are not getting older. Sure they can say 'I have a good plastic surgeon', and he might make sixty look like twenty nine. But someday the jig is up. And if the humans know, they must go or be eaten. That's why I don't act. I have been in the business almost fifty years now. And its time I die. Or as you well know, it's time to reinvent myself. How about you Victor?"

"About every fifty or sixty years Nightfire and I move on. And wherever the vamps are I inject myself. Wars, earthquakes, floods, genocides, wherever they go to feast and lust for blood, I am there. Because, of course you know, they all must die."

Victor changed subjects abruptly. "Barnaby, how long has your butler been with you?"

"Twenty five years. Why do you ask?"

"Because he smells of vampire and I don't mean you."

"If not me then who?"

"It could be he just rubbed against one in the market or hallway."

"Man Victor, you always had a great power. Truly you have gifts other vampires don't have. Robert always smelled like Brut to me." Barnaby took another short draw on his glass and called out, "Robert, come in here please,"

"Yes Mister Barnaby?" The butler said as he stood just inside the doorway.

"My friend here is a very special... person. How long have you worked for me Robert?"

"Almost twenty five years Sir."

"Robert, how long have you been a spy?"

"A spy Sir?"

"Yes Robert, a spy for the vampires."

"I would say twenty five years, Sir!" Robert looked gleeful and relieved to have finally dropped the charade.

Robert drew a 45 automatic pistol and fired two shots before Victor sliced him in half. But it was too late for Barnaby. The first shot was a head shot. And Barnaby simply went up in ash, then fell to dust.

Victor sensed vamps and a lot of them. He made for the door and as he opened it he could see the hallway was already dark with vamps flickering toward the apartment. Victor went to the window. As the vamps came through the door into the darkened room, Victor waited. Then when the room was full of vampires he ripped down the curtain to fill the room with sunlight. The room quickly became full of smoke and ash, then dust. Victor made his way to the stairwell. He knew it would be a fight all the way down. He could not help but feel he had gotten his friend killed. At least now Barnaby had found rest. At least now he could be with his sister Kendra.

Victor opened the door to the stairwell. "Alright you vamps! COME GET SOME!" he grabbed the handrail as two vampires reached the landing. With a vertical slice the two vampires slipped into quarters then ash. As Victor leapt over the rail, vamps on every floor were reaching for him. As he descended he swung his sword wildly with large slashes, and hands, arms, faces and heads fell with him until they turned to ash. Victor landed, rolled up on his feet, and out into the lobby where Frankie and the clerk were.

Victor yelled, "OUTSIDE! NOW!" But it was too late. At least ten vampires were circling the walls and ceiling. Victor pulled his Colts and began firing. The vamps overran the clerk. He yelled at Frankie to get outside again, all the while continuously firing until the guns were empty. But the vampires kept coming. The hotel was infested with them. Frankie and Victor ran for the door. A vampire dropped straight down on Frankie and took a large bite from his face and neck. Victor spun around and around with his sword. There were so many. He was up to his knees in dust and it was getting hard to walk in it. Finally he reached the door, kicked it open into the afternoon sunlight.

"Burn you sons of vampires, burn!"

He made his way to the truck. Once inside he watched as vamps continued coming out and bursting into flames, but the onslaught could not reach him. Something powerful was driving them, compelling them to come out into the sun. He was sure it had to be their master.

Victor pulled the big rig back onto the I-5 Freeway and headed north. He had a hunch that it would be to the north where he would find Contesa Vargas.

CHAPTER FOURTEEN

SO FAR THE WHOLE TRIP had been a loss of extreme magnitude. First Sabrina, then Barnaby, and some good humans. Victor hadn't collected any flesh or blood samples yet. And he needed vampire blood or flesh badly for his genetic experiments, so as to continue trying to duplicate the gene sequence. Bio-engineering was the next logical step. By introducing and engineering genes that would reformulate the gene sequence itself. Victor had already been successful in changing bovine blood to human blood. Some of the bovines produced type A and type B blood. The exact type a human would need in a transfusion. Once the genetic code was built Victor would introduce it to the vampire population.

In other words the queen or head vampires would be loaded up on the new geno-code, rendering his or her genetic code obsolete. Voila! No more vampire.

Victor would track more vamps for the sample he needed to take back to his laboratory on his ranch in Montana.

The sky began to darken close to the grapevine on I-5. Victor was running infrared and radar to spot any vampire movement. The big rig shook and rumbled up the interstate. Victors mind was wandering. He could not shake the feeling of loss of his friend Barnaby. Almost two hundred years Barnaby had been alive and in one day with Victor, he was dead.

As Victor started down the grapevine there were several beeps on the radar. They were headed north, close to the ground, then they were gone. He down shifted for a long grade. Six percent for three miles. He eased 'The Pete' down the slope. Once in the valley close to Bakersfield the radar and sonar were going wild. Vamps were running rampant through this area.

Victor pulled the truck off of the freeway into a truck stop. Victor calculated the closest vamp to where he was. That part was easy. As the night wore on, more and more vampires were in the sky. Some would flicker through the truck stop looking for any victims to feast upon.

He had parked toward the back of the lot. Catching a vampire sounded easier than it was. They were constantly moving at a high rate of speed, flickering in and out of sight. They swarmed together most of the time. Only because Victor was a vampire could he see them. He would have to make his move when one or two strayed from the swarm.

A young female vamp flickered by the truck after Victor had put out some bovine blood by the back of the trailer. As soon as she was close he hit his disrupter on his belt buckle and with that the vampire stopped in her tracks long enough for Victor to lasso her and extract some blood and flesh. The whole process took less than thirty seconds. Then he sliced off her head and watched with satisfaction as ash and dust fell.

Through his studies, Victor had discovered that usually there were two or three "thinking vampires" in a swarm, but not always. Sometimes there would be a nest close by where the vampires could be protected from sunlight and venture out at night like this swarm.

This was a good spot. He had collected five samples. It was time to go. But first Victor would booby trap some blood. He poured it on the ground into a gallon sized puddle with trip wires connected to an ultraviolet light grenade. Boom! Flash! Nobody knows.

As Victor started the big rig he watched as vampires swarmed the puddle of blood. First two, then five, until a large crowd gathered. It looked like a bonfire at the beach when the grenade exploded. It was very bright but only lasted a second.

Victor rolled north. He would stay on I-5 collecting more samples. A warning light began to flash on the dashboard. Something was attacking his security! He checked his mirrors. Vampires alright! They had landed on the truck like flies. "They're probably attracted to the bovine blood", Victor thought to himself. He activated the truck defenses which put out a burst of 500,000 volts through the truck and trailer. Nightfire and the livestock were insulated from electrocution. The vampires were popping like popcorn creating a slight amber of ash caught in the wind. Finally the small swarm veered off toward the east.

Victor studied the big rig in the cameras and disarmed its security system. Daylight would be making its way into the valley. The bright glow of the sun would force any vampire into the dark shadows, into their dirt sarcophaguses where vampires take refuge. For in the light their bodies would burn as would their souls in hell with no chance for rest hereafter.

CHAPTER FIFTEEN

AS VICTOR MOVED INTO NORTHERN California he thought of old times when it took him a week to travel from Los Angeles to Stockton, now only hours. As he looked out the window at people moving so fast, he felt like he was moving so slow. It was always dark in the cab. Looking out at the world was so bright. He was often overcome with loneliness, wanting to be at rest. And the companionship of humans was not in his reach. Four hundred sixty years with only a few brilliant sparks of humanity. And this, his family as a child and young adult. Kendra; a flash of love so bright his heart would always glow. To honor his humanity, and the ones he loved; this is what Victor drew strength upon to keep fighting vampires until the day he died. He might be a vampire with a cursed soul, but never the less a soul.

And a human soul with compassion for a good human is worth ten thousand soulless vampires.

So revenge would be his companion through life. The sadness was just the shadow of his revenge. Loneliness was just a preparation for the war he was waging on the world. A war Victor Jane did not intend to lose.

Late afternoon a strip of sunlight loomed burnt orange, but the darkness was beginning to crush it from the east. Victor pulled the truck into a truck stop for fuel. The truck had two, one hundred fifty gallon tanks, but it still need to be fueled. He went through his routine checks for the truck; tires, water, oil. He wanted to be back on the road as soon as possible and well into Oregon country by morning. Nightfire needed time out of the truck and so did the cattle.

At U.S. 97 just north of Bend Oregon, Victor pulled the big rig onto a dirt road. Two miles ahead was the Bent Bar B Ranch. This is where he would rest the livestock. The "B" was deserted. It was also Victors. He had bought it in 1900. It was only one of numerous out of the way properties he owned. The title now showed that it belonged to the Jane family's great grandson, Victor Jane. He hadn't been there for twenty years. Victor pulled the truck next to the corral. It need some work. Victor would fix it tomorrow.

As the sun rose the following day it revealed that the whole place needed a lot of work. Victor tackled the coral first and put the cattle in it. Then he secured the barn. Surprisingly it wasn't in too bad of shape. Then some house cleaning to get settled in. The livestock, Nightfire, and the truck were put away.

The trucks security perimeter included the house, barn, and corral. Victor needed this. He could never know when vampires might attack. There hadn't been a sound on the radar or sonar, and here in the back country not too much to feast on. The population was sparse and not a lot of out and out killing going on.

That evening Victor had already started some experiments on the blood samples he had collected. Some of the tissue was put into petri dishes to grow. Several different compounds would be mixed and added to them. The idea was to create a serum that could be absorbed by the cells themselves. Dopamine and serotonin are chemicals that cause reactions in the cell at a sub-molecular bio-level. Simply put, they would change, they would act different; they would no longer be a vampire.

It would be a daunting task to reverse the infection in the whole world but Victor had a plan. It would only take one bite to get it started. Victor could see he was a long way off from that day, but it was coming and Victor had lots of time.

With each passing day, their numbers increased. Victor estimated a fifty percent jump in the vampire population in just the last twenty five years. They were getting more and more bold, smart, and the ability to blend in with humans was easy now, like at the truck stop. They could pass by a human and nick the skin and lightly consume their blood like a mosquito. There wasn't a pesticide for vampires. Not yet anyway.

Victor was also working on a disrupter on a bigger scale. One that worked digitally over the cell phone network. By using the cell tower, a large burst would expose the vamps for a short time for all to see. When you can see them you can kill them. There was a lot of work to do.

CHAPTER SIXTEEN

VICTOR SADDLED UP NIGHTFIRE, AND attached all the sun protective gear for the both of them. He would move the cattle to the other side of the ranch and then move them back. The herd needed the exercise so their muscles did not become atrophied from non-movement. And besides, Victor needed to clear his mind and just riding the big stallion was the way to do that. Purple sage covered the ranch along with sugar pine trees. A thing of real beauty of Mother Nature. The ranch itself was about five thousand acres of mostly grassy land and meadows. The mountainous side was mostly sage and pines.

Nightfire was feeling his oats...blood oats that is. Victor put the Lipenstein stallion through his paces with a series of jumps and turns through the country side. Four hundred years of practice had made rider and horse magical together. It was a happy time shared between Victor and Nightfire.

The change of pace brought great relief for both. In centuries past, the trail had been isolated for the two. Months on end travelling with herd, through the wilderness and the rare sighting of a vampire was unusual. In fact there had been a point in time where vampires were virtually non-existent and that Victor and Nightfire were the only ones.

By the fourth day Victor had loaded the cattle and Nightfire aboard the rig and was headed down the dirt road to U.S. 97 North. He was headed home to Montana. There was a lot of work to be done and a lot of vampires to be killed. If he had learned anything over the years it was that all vampires must die! Oregon had always been a beautiful place and Victor did not mind passing through it. As the big rig rolled up the highway to the northern state border at Biggs Oregon he began to sense an uneasiness which usually meant vampires.

He did a quick systems check. The radar was fussy at best because of interference from the mountains he was rolling through. Victor checked the sonar and sent out some pings to see if anything would come back. Yes there it was, a swarm overhead. But Victor couldn't tell if they were following him or just passing over. "Not likely Victor", He told himself, and armed the security system on the truck.

It was a large enough swarm to be concerned. Victor had to get into a more open space. An ambush in this canyon was to their favor. So for now he would play possum as if he hadn't noticed them. Finally the big truck rolled out of the canyons on a long stretch of highway that ran through a little bit of farmland and rocky ground. Victor had an idea. The swarm was pretty high up in the air above him. He would set the frequency of his disrupter to the same frequency as the CB in the truck and use the outside speaker to blast them from the sky. Well, that is if it would work at all! But it was worth a try. It took a few minutes to set it all up, but Victor was an old hand at driving the big Peterbuilt truck and never swerved an inch.

Soon it was ready for a trial. The old college try as they used to say at Gonzaga University where Victor had studied engineering over a century ago. Just one of a few institutions where Victor had studied. It had been a long life and Victor had always been a good student. From Oxford in England to Northwestern for his doctorate in biochemistry and nano physics at MIT.

Victor turned up the volume on his CB radio and hit the handset button. It went out a very high frequency, barely audible, and there they were for all to see. Their malformed faces and bodies hurling through time and space. Most of the vamps were grabbing their heads and flying down out of the air. They began to hit the rocks and ground hard. At that height and speed it was devastating. Heads, arms, and legs, were twisted and torn off. Some were hitting so hard that they burst like a giant blood blister! Some would hit, try to stand straight up, then fall because every bone in their body was broken, but most just turned to jelly. This was followed immediately thereafter by brief amber flashes and then dust and ash.

Victor smiled as a child would watching the bug zapper for the first time.

CHAPTER SEVENTEEN

AS VICTOR ROLLED SLOWLY OFF the highway onto a dirt road which lead to his ranch just outside of Butte, Montana, he thought to himself, "It is good to be home". Victor had made significant strides in the war on vampires this trip. But he knew that new and more drastic measures were going to be needed to win this war. New weapons were needed. New strategies were going to have to be employed. And it was time to attack from the inside out. To begin the end of all vampires to stop the infection at the source, at the heart of evil which preys on the innocent. Victor Jane was just the man...vampire to do that. Because in the dark he saw them. In the sunlight he exposed them and in his humanity he would not fail. They all must die.

–The end...well, for now.–

Book Three

CHAPTER ONE

"...SEVEN, SIX, FIVE, FOUR, THREE, two, one, ignition. Rockets are a go. We have liftoff San Diego. All systems are a go. Fuel level ninety percent. Com link a go. Reaching forty thousand feet Mr. Jane."

"Roger that mission support. Four minutes before docking with Nightfire One. Countdown at one minute Mission Support."

"Roger that Mr. Jane."

The small stratosphere rocket would dock with the larger intergalactic cruiser to take Victor Jane on what might be his last ride.

"One minute, fifty nine, fifty eight, fifty seven", the docking would be tricky but Victor had done it hundreds of times. "Starting to roll into docking Nightfire One. The smaller rocket's engines went silent. Several small retro-rockets fired to bring it into docking position. "Nightfire One, you have the stick."

"Copy Victor". The computer generated voice said.

The smaller rocket touched down onto the interlock port of the Nightfire One. "Docking complete Victor," the ship acknowledged. "Mission Support, confirms docking complete Mr. Jane.", said the voice on the overhead speaker. This time it was a humans' voice, and that voice belonged to Dr. Conrad Bell.

"Conrad?"

"Yes Mr. Jane."

"How long have you known me, seven years? I think you can call me Victor if you like."

"I would like that ever so much."

Professor Bell was an astrophysicist with two Doctorate degrees, one in Advanced Bio-Mechanics, and Astro-plane Particles. He was also the head of Mission Support for Nightfire One's endeavor to save mankind.

The year was 2210. Time had been marching on for Victor Jane. A simple flash in time for humanity. Eight hundred and fifty years old now, Victor Jane still looked twenty five. The old vampire was holding up pretty good for his age.

"Rocket One is secured Victor. Welcome aboard."

"Thanks Nightfire One. Speaking of Nightfire, how is he?"

"Nightfire is well Victor. He arrived last night at nineteen hundred hours and is in hold stall one. Although there was some difficulty moving from Rocket Two to his stall."

"Is everything alright?"

"Yes Victor."

"Yeah, he is nervous about space flight, he and the livestock. But Nightfire will be fine as always. Any problems getting the livestock aboard?"

"No Victor. They are in holding containment two. I will check on them before P.E.C."

"Very well Victor."

"Mission Support, What are my numbers please?"

"You are one hundred percent on P.E.C. Victor." P.E.C. meant Particulate Echo Conversion. The particles of a solid are disassembled and bombed into the echo of light. The conversion takes only milliseconds. When P.E.C. conversion occurs, the particle becomes the echo itself. The echo remains after light has passed through it. You must exit at a calculated point in mass, back to light. The complexity had become fairly routine... if you spend three hundred years formulating it as Victor had. The name Nightflight was given to the entire process.

Thirty seconds, twenty nine, twenty eight,...After all the years Victor spent working on Nightflight it was finally time to soar. Eighteen, seventeen, sixteen...Victor locked himself into pilot command located at the forward end of Nightfire One's main controls. The vessel itself was massive, the size of a small city. It had taken thirty years to build it and a cost of trillions of dollars. Also there had been millions of man hours required, and most of Earth's population to construct it. Literally every man, woman and child not infected had worked or sacrificed part of themselves for the building of Nightfire One. Nine, eight, seven, six,...

In the year 2083 Earths world leaders came together to create a unified front against the vampire scourge that was killing Earths people. But it had taken a lot of convincing from Victor. Vampires were shown as a plague on Earth and if not stopped, humanity as we knew it would cease to exist. Vampires were in every country. The world leaders formed a consortium to address the pandemic that was slowly killing Earth. Victor was the foremost authority on vampirism, him being a vampire. He had the right answers. Victor had the only answers. The vampires must all die if humanity were to live. Three, two, one!

Victor soon realized he had touched every fabric of being of matter. Light, darkness, and echo. The galaxy cruiser appeared as quickly as it had disappeared.

"Nightfire One, to Mission Support, come in?" A silent few moments passed as com links were established.

"Yes Victor, we hear you. Are you okay?"

"As far as I can tell Conrad." Loud yells erupted throughout Mission Support. Over one hundred years were put into this project. The humans were fighting a losing battle against the vampires. Only small resistance groups remained. It was very dangerous to travel outside of a guarded city such as San Diego.

"All systems a go on our end Victor."

"Professor McCall has found a convergence in compartment C on the third level. She thinks it might be white noise from nano construction during the hulls fabrication."

"Roger that Conrad. I will run a diagnostic and Conrad, tell Professor McCall good job as usual."

"Thank you Victor." A female voice came back over the intercom. Professor McCall was the leading nano-molecular engineer and astrophysicist, and had been on the Nightfire One construction project for six years. At twenty seven she was the most intelligent human Victor had ever met. She held masters degrees from three major universities. If that wasn't enough she could have been Miss America or a model. She was stunning and Victor had been taken with her from the very first moment he laid eyes on her. At five foot nine with blonde hair and striking blue eyes when she talked she could hold an entire room in silence. Victor had thought there may be something between them but whatever it was would have to wait. They were there to do a job. The most important job of all time, to save humanity.

CHAPTER TWO

NIGHTFIRE ONE SAT ONE THOUSAND miles outside Saturn's rings. Victor could see Valgor. That was the name of the planet the vampires had come from. It could not be seen with a telescope, but scientists had found it with galaxy probes. The planet itself carried the vibration signature of a vampire. It was a small planet about one eighth the size of Earth. Cold, dark gray in color, the planet was made up mostly of iron. There was an atmosphere and some water, but the planet Valgor did not receive light. It was in line with the dark side of Saturn.

"Nightfire One. Map out vibrations on the planet."

"Yes Victor," the ship replied.

Victor's journey onto the cold planet would be within the hour. Even with the protection of the rings of Saturn, Victor was exposed to possible attack. Vampires, as far as Victor knew, did not have a vehicle in which they travelled. They either leapt or flickered and somehow traveled along their vibration, or the vibration of light. Anyhow, he must beware.

"Victor the vibration maps are complete and downloaded onto your com link."

"Thank you Nightfire One. Run diagnostic and system check."

"Vibration anomaly in hull, compartment three C." The answer came back.

"Okay. I will check it out."

"Security set at one hundred percent Victor."

"Copy that Nightfire One."

Victor made his way to the ship's onboard armory before going to the holding corrals aboard Nightfire One. Being in space meant having an all new class of weapons. Victor's silver sword would still make the trip to the surface of Valgor along with a laser pistol, light grenades, and a hyper-fire laser rifle, plus one special disrupter belt. Victor left the armory to load

Nightfire aboard Rocket One. The stallion would accompany Victor to the planet.

"Well this is it old friend." Victor said softly in Nightfire's ear. "Our journeys end is close. And if it is to be our last, then we shall travel it together." Victor and the stallion could survive the planet. They were vampires. Victor prepared Nightfire for the battle. Complete body armor for the stallion with his own disrupter with a 500,000 volt vampire rejecter. They could look but not touch.

Victor and Nightfire had ridden together a million miles. The great stallion meant Victors entire being. From his dreams, his family and Victor's love. The stallion had been there for wars, for heartbreak, for recreation, and stood true, upright, and bold in the face of destruction just to be a loyal friend and companion through the centuries. Nightfire was a reminder of who Victor was eight hundred and fifty years ago; a horseman. And Nightfire was the finest horse on the planet Earth, and now in the galaxy.

Victor looked into the stallion's eyes, patted him on the neck plating, and asked, "Are you ready boy? Alright." He said as Nightfire shook his head as if in response.

As Victor loaded the great stallion aboard Rocket One, a voice came over his com link implant. "Victor?"

"Yes Conrad?"

"The imploders have been activated."

The imploders were planet killers, with an explosion designed to cause a planet to implode on itself. The idea was to destroy the planet Valgor so the spread of vampirism would no longer be a threat.

Once Nightfire was loaded aboard Rocket One and secured, Victor made his way to compartment three section C where the anomaly had been detected. The door opened and a soft light came on. The compartment held two particle bombarders, relay units, and some large conduits.

Victor's senses were on high alert. Vamps! just as he had thought.

A vampire leaped from behind one of the units. Victor moved to his right as he fell back, and grabbed the vamp's jacket by the shoulder. He used the momentum to propel the vamp into the wall, mashing its face and neck into jelly. A second vampire flickered down from the ceiling. Victor lashed out with a hard right kick that caught the vamp in the solar plexus and drove him flat against the ceiling. As Victor landed on his feet he threw a side kick to the first vampire's neck which pinched it right off the vamps shoulders. As it fell from the ceiling, Victor moved quickly across the floor, sword drawn to the opposite side on the compartment. As he did the vamp was relieved of his head. Both vampires glowed of orange amber in the green soft light of the compartment.

"Stop vampire killer!, a voice called out, "Stop please!"

A young woman stood up from the corner of the compartment. "Please do not kill me. I do not want to be a vampire!" She held her hand up as if to protect herself. Victor somehow found that gesture to be human, and his humanity moved him to stop.

"Who are you?" Demanded Victor.

She started to cry. "I am Layla. My name is Layla!"

"What are you doing here with these vampires?"

"I live here", the young girl said. She looked to be thirteen or fourteen. "I have lived here for some months. Nobody had noticed us til now. Those two were my friends that you killed!"

"They attacked me," Victor said.

"You would have killed them anyway!", She sobbed, "We just wanted to be safe!"

"Layla, you're infected. You're a vampire!"

"I don't want to be a vampire! This was not my *CHOICE*! Was it your choice?!" The young girl screamed.

Victor felt eight hundred years of pain and suffering all at once. A great soul wrenching shock. The vampire man knew what she said to be true. There had been vampires throughout Victor's life that were still mostly human. Like his friend Barnaby Collingsworth. Even Nightfire had been good and true. Victor had seen that all vampires were to die, but what to do with this one?

Victor turned and began to walk away. The young looking vampire made her move, lunging at Victor's neck from behind. Victor simply raised his sword up and at an angle. The vampire Layla impaled herself on it. Victor felt her small hands on his shoulders before she burst into flames. Her light lit the room for a moment then darkness.

Victor knew it was wrong for him to hesitate, that he had let himself feel human. He could not afford to be human. He was about to land of

Valgor where he would have to be anything but human.

"Mission Support? Are there anymore variances in vibrations on Nightfire One?"

"No Victor. You have fixed the problem."

"Okay, Conrad? I am on my way to Rocket One."

Victor made his way to the ships cockpit, a small control room where Victor began analyzing data from the planet of vampires. Valgor was cold with temperatures in the upper 30's (F) in most parts of the planet. Its surface winds were at a steady forty miles an hour. Valgor had an inner core much like Earth which kept the planet from freezing completely. The entire planet was a maze of underground tunnels and caves with several superstructures above ground. Systems showed a large concentration of vampires were heavier at these points on the planet. Victor would land in a small valley closest to the largest of the superstructures in hopes of not being seen. The whole mission was dependent upon it. All of Earth depended on it.

CHAPTER THREE

"THREE, TWO, ONE, LAUNCH COMPLETE Victor. Rocket One is away."

"Roger that control."

The ship started a slow motion barrel roll from underneath Nightfire One. The rocket would complete some small maneuvers to bring it into Valgor's orbit. Rocket One would travel under the ring of Saturn so as not to be detected, but appeared to be floating debris from the rings themselves. The whole trip would take about one hour.

"Mission Support, plot a course to Valgor."

It was important to get all of the debris recorded so Victor didn't fly into a big rock that had drifted from the rings of Saturn.

"Yes Victor. We have coordinates for you uploaded to com link on Rocket One."

"Roger that Mission Support."

Rocket One would reach a speed of two thousand miles per hour before dropping into Valgor's orbit. It would be ten minutes until landing on the surface. Victor watched as a large asteroids stood as sentinels to Saturn. Some were as big as five miles across and were solid ice and dust that had collected in space. The sun reflected a brilliant shade of white and silver blue with orange outlines against a black backdrop of space. As one asteroid collided with another, light refractions through the minute particles caused Rocket One to appear as if bathed in blue velvet. As the vampire mans eyes wondered at the spectacle the intercom interrupted.

"All systems are a go here Victor."

"Roger that Conrad."

"Victor, how's the weather on Valgor?"

"Like we predicted."

"Mission Support, please bring all of Nightfire Ones weapon array online."

"Copy that Victor."

Nightfire One had many types of weapons. Laser guided cannons which were activated by Victor through an implanted com link that allowed him to point and shoot. It was also equipped with twenty interspace imploding missiles. Each missile was capable of taking out ten square feet to ten square miles. All were adjusted by Victor's optic implants. All this technology was so when Victor was in battle he was in control of Nightfire Ones impressive weapons systems. Radar, sonar, infrared, and motion sensors were all built into his com link, implanted behind his left ear.

Rocket One emerged from under the rings of Saturn, now on a glide toward Valgor. "Ten minutes and counting until touchdown Victor."

"Roger Mission Support."

The small rocket fired a retro booster to slow the descent. Victor looked out the observation window at Valgor's purplish gray surface and thought to himself, 'A dead planet with a soulless race of beings.' Vampires had infected Earth to the point of almost no return.

Vampires had murdered Victors family and his friends and now after eight hundred and fifty years it was coming to an end, one way or another.

"T minus two minutes Victor."

"Roger Mission Support. Nightfire One, you have the controls."

The retro rockets fired simultaneously and Rocket One touched down on the planet Valgor like a feather floating to the ground.

"All engines off. All security systems online for Rocket One."

"Roger that Mission Support."

The small ship would sit ready in sleep mode. "No short range vibration detected Victor. However there is a major movement of Vampires ten miles due east. It looks like a line of red army ants moving toward the target superstructure."

"Okay Mission Support, I have them on my com link." Victor could see the vampires on his target viewfinder. It looks as if the vamps were climbing over one another in a line maybe five miles long.

Victor moved toward the holding compartment for his stallion but first he would be stopping by the ships armory. Victor looked the same as he did in the old days in young America. A black cowboy hat, black duster, black boots, but all with a space-age high density micro polymer with nano particulate construction. It was laser and bullet proof, and from head to toe it adhered to Victor's body. It was also self contained air and had gas filtration systems. Nightfire also had the same systems in place if needed.

CHAPTER FOUR

"THE ATMOSPHERE IS SUSTAINABLE VICTOR." It was the voice of Professor Lori McCall over his com link. "Temperature is a steady forty one degrees with the wind."

"Thanks Professor."

"I think you can call me Lori if you would like."

"I think I would. Thanks Lori."

She continued, "We will be monitoring vampire movement and relaying the information as best we can. With the subspace disturbance it won't be much."

"Copy that Profess...I meant Lori."

The Mission Support team smiled to each other. They knew their survival was in the vampire spaceman's hands. They were counting on the man part to get it done.

Nightfire One would be the eyes and ears for Victor while he was on the planet's surface. Small transmitters would relay information from the surface to Victor and back to Nightfire One via Rocket One. The cannon would take a few seconds after firing. The missiles would take one to two minutes. Victor did not want to fire and then move. He may shoot himself. In the end they would implode the planet, but first they needed all of the information about the vampire planet. It was possible Valgor may not be the only one. Earth also needed to know how the vampires were getting from place to place through space.

Victor and Nightfire disembarked the ship. Victor gave the command, "stealth mode". The ship was undetectable by sight or sound. The big black Lipenstein stallion felt as at home here as he had at home in France with Jewels, Victor's sister. Or with Victor in their home in Montana. I felt good to be back in the saddle. There hadn't been much riding for the pair as there had been in the old days.

A century had passed as Victor prepared humanity and Earth for these few hours in space. The journey had been a long and arduous one. The science alone took decades. The construction took another century. Three and four generations had worked on the project. It all rested on the vampire spaceman.

The Planets terrain was mucky and hard to keep traction but Nightfire had always been surefooted and strong. It was in his nature. Victor and the big black horse headed east where the last record of vamps had been taken.

It wouldn't be hard to find them. Along with video and coms Victor could smell them. The lower mindless types were always flickering in and out of range. Victor was beginning to sense vampires overhead. Not many, but one or two. Victor reined Nightfire to a halt and watched as the two vampires passed closer. The pair looked grayish, almost black, much like the color of the planet itself. Their cloths looked to be torn, but as they drew closer still Victor saw that they wore uniforms. Black shirts with openings in the back for their wings. As their elongated faces, large eyes, sunken noses, drew even closer, Victor could tell they would see him.

At that very moment, the vampire on the left side screeched. At the same time Victor fired twice from his laser rifle. The Light Accelerator 2000 took the vamps down from 1000 feet out. The thick air caused the vampires to burn a little longer as they trailed into dust and floated to the ground. Victor knew he was headed in the right direction.

The planet's surface became rockier with some vegetation and a sparsely wooded area where the trees looked like dead stone slightly swaying in the wind. A constant mist passed through the air. The combination of wind and mist made a sound of a high pitch whistle as it whipped through the trees.

Victors recon intel from Nightfire One was showing large concentrations of vamps just over the next small rise. Victor's optical implant gave a heads up real time view on command. Nightfire One could see the data on a dime at two thousand miles above the planet.

He dismounted just before the top of the rise by a small outcropping of rock. From Victor's vantage point he could see the large superstructure made from the stone of the planet. Square at the bottom then a round sphere in the middle with a particularly large opening at the top. There was one entrance as far as Victor could tell.

"Nightfire One, give me a structural 360 diagram."

"Yes Victor." The voice said in his com link implant.

A moment later his optical monitor showed a digital map of the structure. It was ten stories high and three stories deep. The digital readout on the heads up display showed many levels with a large central room in the middle of the sphere itself.

The swarm on the ground twisted and heaved back and forth one vamp to another, passing what looked like flesh dripping with blood. Most climbed from head to toe as they climbed over each other passing in and out of the superstructure. Some of the vamps were carrying the flesh in their mouths and others had the bloody meat-like substance in their claws moving in an uncontrolled column which stretched for miles across the surface of the planet. A trail of vampire feces and urine permeated the air.

"Nightfire One. Where does the column begin."

"Victor, the columns start underground about fourteen miles northwest of your location. Several smaller columns combine into one larger column."

"Copy Nightfire One."

Victor would need a slight distraction to gain access to the superstructure. Mid level overseers were spaced every half mile or so, watching the underlings travel through the column.

"Nightfire One. Laser array. Target one hundred feet of column leading into the superstructure and all aerial targets within one half mile of the entrance."

"Targets locked Victor."

"On my mark Nightfire One."

"Yes Victor."

Victor's plan was to get in and out as fast as possible. Victor dismounted Nightfire.

"Stay here boy. I'm going to need you for a fast getaway, okay?"

Victor armed the black stallion's armor and security system. Aboard his saddle which gave Victor sight and sound to see and command Nightfire. Moving through the mist two hundred yards from the entrance, he could see the column pulsating. He decided to flicker the last one hundred yards and gave the command, "FIRE!"

The flash was instant. The first one hundred yards of the column disappeared and the vampires that were leaping into the air were gone as well. Just small embers and dust were falling to the ground. Victor was in.

The column quickly reformed as if nothing had happened. The entrance was large, about forty feet square. Once inside Victor could see a purplish light which emanated from the passageway. He moved quickly along the wall. Vampires were everywhere; walls, floor, and ceiling, moving rapidly. Some were even flickering across Victor. His suit began to turn red from the fleshy meat-like substance the vamps were carrying. They moved, aware of Victor even though the overseers were focused on the prize, the bloody meat. They seemed completely absorbed in their purpose of moving the meat to its destination. Victor began dropping transponders to mark his way out of the superstructure when the time came.

After a short distance the passageway opened into a large chamber which had narrow, flat walkways leading upward. Victor counted twenty two of these ramps. He kept to the wall and started up the first ramp. It spiraled up five or six stories. Once he had reached the top the pathway entered a long dimly lit hall. It was seven feet tall and six feet wide with hooks along one wall. Five feet up below the hooks were troughs. The meat was brought, hung, and the blood was drained into the trough. The old bloody rancid meat was being replaced by fresh bloody meat. Vampires with paddles pushed the blood down the trough to a center drain. As best Victor could tell the vamps would exit at the end of the passageway, and return to the column. Victor continued transponders as he made his way through the structure. In a low voice he said, "Nightfire One. Copy."

A moments pause, "Yes Victor. Your com link is eight-six percent."

"I need visual diagram from my position".

Two seconds later it appeared on Victor's optical monitor in his right viewer. It showed a large maze of pathways spiraling up the sphere and down the hallways then back down to the entrance. With a single substructure below the sphere and a large opening above the sphere which had two pathways to the substructure. The diagram also showed the plumbing at work. It was all draining down to the sub chamber. Victor had to go up to go down.

He was amazed the vamps paid no attention to him whatsoever and the overseers were nonexistent inside the structure. A pathway ran in a circle around the opening at the top before ascending back down to the entrance.

As Victor got closer a vampire came in through the opening, folded his wings in, turned and gave a cautious look behind him and started down through an opening to a round sided tunnel, one of two. Victor waited a few moments then followed the vampire down. He was careful to move quietly. The pathway was lit in red crystals. There was some sort of glow in the dark below. As he descended the pathway the vampire in front had stopped. Victor drew his laser pistol. And as Victor turned the next corner the vamp was standing there looking at him surprised and angry. Victor quelled his temper with the short blast of his pistol. Amber and dust enveloped the hallway. Victor could hear vampires coming up the pathway but he didn't know how many.

"Nightfire One!"

"Yes Victor."

"All systems opti-view heads up!"

"Yes Victor."

The image appeared. There were four vamps coming right at him from thirty feet down. Victor moved quickly down the pathway to engage. The vamps were startled to say the least. Four shot, four hit. Some of the amber floated along the ceiling as most of the dust hit the floor. The viewer showed that Victor had had to move seven stories down. The pathway was silent except for sounds from above; the shuffle of vamps in and out of the superstructure.

"Victor, you are one floor above the bottom chamber."

"Thanks Nightfire One."

Victor moved slowly down into the opening of the massive chamber. He assessed the room's contents. The heads-up view finder showed six vampires and humans, and some things Victor could not identify. A slow voice said, "Come in V-I-C-T-O-O-O-R. We have been waiting a long, long time for YOOOU!"

Victor stepped into the open chamber. It was lit with the same glowing red light of the hallway, but brighter. Blood dripped from the ceiling into a large center fountain. There were two vampires drinking from the fountain.

Two more vampires were hunched next to what appeared to be two thrones. The oldest looking vampire Victor had ever seen sat at the throne, and now spoke to Victor. Contessa Vargas sat upon the other. Two humans sat at her feet. Contessa's arm, severed by Victor centuries ago, had grown back. "Father, I told you he would come. How long has it been Victor?" Contessa mockingly said.

"Not long enough to cleanse my nose of your vile smell Contessa!" She leaned forward with a hiss.

The old vampire spoke. "Calm yourself my daughter." He began to move in a circle around Victor. "Have you brought us a present Victor? Have you brought the Stallion of Lipenstein to us?"

Victor found the comment funny, and Victor rarely found anything funny.

"Yes I have brought the black Lipenstein Stallion", and with that comment Victor drew his sword. "But that is not the present I brought you VAMPIRE!"

The old vampire croaked, "Please, Victor, call me Father. Or if you wish you may call me Alu! That is my name. I am the father of all vampires. I am twice the age of Christ himself. I have fed upon Earth since troglodytes. Humans! They are a treat!

"You see Victor, there are a hundred just like me throughout the universe and all the galaxies. We are the evil. Millenniums ago the deal was made. I was given Earth." Contessa smiled madly holding back her sick laughter from Alu's zealous comment.

"And who dealt you the Earth, Alu?!" Victor demanded.

"Why God of course."

The two vampires moved even closer to Victor. "Alu, if God had given you the Earth, you would not be hiding out here in space. Cold, dark and scared!"

The old vampires eyes tightened and his expression changed dramatically to one of anger. "SILENCE INSOLENT CHILD!" He thundered.

"How do you get around to Earth and back with that old rat-like body?"

Instantly Victor found himself hanging from the wall. Just like a flash the old vampire held Victor fast to the wall. Victor could not move. Contessa moved in and pinned his arms and legs. The old vampire struck

Victor and the lights went out.

The next thing Victor knew was awakening to the sound of chains rattling...chains that bound him. Stripped down to his trousers, his head felt as if a train had run over it. The old vampire was fast and strong. As soon as Victor got his senses back he could hear, "Victor...Victor...This is Nightfire One. Come in Victor."

"Yes Nightfire One. This is Victor." He could barely get the words out.

"Set the laser array to heads up viewfinder. Target vampires."

"Yes Victor".

Two of the vamps came close to see what Victor was saying. One of the vampires grabbed Victor by the face. "What are you saying?"

"I said FIRE!!!"

A burst from the laser canon found its mark. Two of the six were ignited into flames. Victor yelled again, "FIRE!" He targeted his chained wrists. "FIRE!" The two laser beams sliced through the ceiling with pinpoint accuracy. The coupling that held him exploded.

Alu was on him again. He threw both fists under the old vampires chin and sent him flying up and back. Victor looked down to the shackle. "FIRE!" Two more laser blasts erupted and Victor was free.

Just as Alu recovered, Victor hit him again full force with all of his body and drove Alu into the stone wall. There was a loud thud as Alu's body impacted one inch deep in the stone wall.

Victor was trying to regain all of his strength. As he staggered backward he felt a sharp pain in his right side. One of the humans that had witnessed all this and was still in the room, had stabbed him with a dagger. If it had been his left side he would be dead now. But that didn't change the fact that it hurt like hell! Being a vampire didn't make him impervious to pain. It always hurt like hell! Victor removed the long knife. The human moved backward away from him. With his back turned, Alu struck Victor with a hard back hand that sent him across the room against the throne. As the old vampire moved in for the kill, Victor threw a side kick as hard as he could that caught Alu on the left side of his neck and jaw. The vampires head spun one hundred eighty degrees and as Alu turned around, Victor jumped with a kick to the bottom of Alu's spine. With a loud snap the old vampire bent backward toward Victor. With one slash of the dagger, Alu's head rolled into ash, then dust. With a flick of the dagger Victor caught the human who had stabbed him, directly in the heart. Victors aim had always been better than a humans.

Contessa was gone and so was the other human. As soon as Victor regained his whereabouts, he retrieved his clothes from a heap nearby the thrones.

"Nightfire One."

"Yes Victor."

"Where is Contessa and the human?"

"They are exiting the superstructure. Shall I target her?"

"No, not yet."

"Victor, there are hundreds of vampires in the superstructure."

"Okay.", Victor thought quickly, "Give me a twenty five foot target radius. Target anything within that space, and fry it!"

Victor dressed and started out of the chamber. Vamps were also starting out of the chamber. They were starting to swarm. As he moved upward the vampires started to ignite and burn...ash and dust. The flash from the laser cannon looked like a strobe, and the more vampires came into the light, at times it looked like the beam was a solid column.

The superstructure began to fall to pieces. Every time a flash came another hole in the ceiling or wall appeared. As Victor ran from the building, it collapsed.

Vampires from the column began to move in every direction. Many of them turned on each other tearing, biting and clawing. A group of overseers were gathered in one tight group. Victor targeted a missile at the group with a one hundred foot radius. Quietly Victor said, "Fire."

Less than one minute later the missiles found their target. Steam and smoke and dust was all that was left.

CHAPTER FIVE

VICTOR MADE HIS WAY TO the rise where Nightfire was waiting. He climbed aboard and reared the big black stallion toward Rocket One.

"Mission Support!"

"Yes Victor."

"I need you to check the record as far back as you can on the reference, Alu."

"Yes Victor. Okay. Give us a minute."

"Relay it to Rocket One." Then to himself he muttered, "We're getting ready to blow this popsicle stand."

"What was that Victor?"

"Nothing Mission Support. Just an old saying."

"Roger Victor."

Sometimes Victor forgot and dated himself. The term popsicle stand was at least three hundred years old. He laughed to himself. The second time today. He must have hit his funny bone.

Victor and Nightfire made their way through the muddy wet mist covered lands of Valgor. Had Alu been truthful about God giving him Earth to feed on? Victor didn't believe it for one minute. Unfortunately he had not learned very much about that. Now he would implode the planet once he and Rocket One were clear. But where was Contessa?

"Nightfire One."

"Yes Victor."

"The vampire Contessa. Where is she?"

"I don't know Victor. She and the humans disappeared about one hundred yards north of the superstructure. I detected an energy burst, and she was gone."

"An energy burst?"

"Yes. Charged particles in the atmosphere."

Victor thought she made it away again using some sort of particle transport beam much like Nightflight. Had Contessa always had this power? For centuries Victor had chased her to no avail. Was this how she had eluded him?

"Nightfire One."

"Yes Victor."

"How many vamps on Valgor?"

"312,682."

"Okay, thanks Nightfire One. Any other humans?"

"Yes Victor. There are four."

"Where are they?"

"Two kilometers due east and just below the surface."

"Copy." Victor reigned Nightfire due east. "Come on boy. Let's go have a look-see shall we?" With that he spurred the big black into a full run.

It took five minutes before Victor saw what looked like a concrete box.

"Heads up on vamps, Nightfire One."

"Yes Victor."

Victor dismounted Nightfire. "Stay boy.", Then Victor made his way into the doorway. "Infrared," Ordered Victor. The humans lit up. They were in the corner. "Who are you and what are you doing here? Victor demanded.

There was a pause then an answer. "Food. We are food."

"Not anymore," Replied Victor. "Come out here."

There was a man, a woman and two children.

"Is this your family?" Victor asked the man.

"No, she and I were brought here separately. The children were already here."

"We must go," said Victor. "There are too many vampires for us to handle. Nightfire One, target vamps one hundred feet."

"Yes Victor."

The man was big eyed, "Who are you mister?"

"My name is Victor Jane, but this is no time for chat. We've got to go."

Outside Victor put the woman and two children on Nightfire. "My horse can't carry us all. What's your name?"

"Jonathan."

"Okay John, you and I will make a run for it. Let's go!" Victor yelled.

The small group headed west for Rocket One. They were still two miles away. The four humans looked gaunt and weak.

"Can you make it two miles John?", Victor asked?

"I don't think so. No water or food since Earth I think."

"What do you mean 'you think'?"

"Because that's where I last remember being before the concrete building."

"Okay," Victor said, "Save your strength."

Nightfire was having no trouble carrying the woman and children, but Jonathan was having a hard time of it. Victor had to help him along. And to make matters worse Victors senses were starting to go off!

"Vampires are headed this way. Here, take this laser pistol." Said Victor as he handed it to Jonathan. "Do you know how to use that?"

"No."

"Just point and shoot!", Victor said.

"Nightfire One."

"Yes Victor."

"Target incoming vampires. Fire at will!"

"Yes Victor."

As the little group continued flashes of light began to rain down out of the air; More and more, closer and closer. The flashes from the laser cannon were almost continuous, but still some vamps were getting through. "Here they come!", Victor yelled.

Victor heaved two light grenades which burst as brilliant as the Sun. Vampires were burning all around the group. Victor and Jonathan had the laser pistols and firing wide open. "There!" Victor yelled, "Ride for the opening!"

The big stallion turned for the opening and charged through. Victor and Jonathan were close behind. The traction was treacherous. Jonathan slipped and fell. In an instant the vampires were upon him. The laser pistol kept firing. Vamps were turning to amber and dust all around him. Then the firing just stopped. Jonathan was gone. Victor lobbed another grenade into the middle of the pile where Jonathan now lay dead. Flash! Burn! The vampires were a flame, then dust.

Nightfire had stopped and was waiting for Victor. "Okay boy." Victor mounted the stallion. "You can do it." The great stallion struggled under the weight but with Victor aboard he would still make it.

The flash from the laser cannon began to slow some, which meant it was keeping up with the attack. Rocket One soon came into sight. There were vamps crawling all over the ship! Somehow, in spite of the cloaking device, the vampires had found it and were working to get in.

"Cargo doors open Rocket One!" Victor ordered.

Horse and riders were immediately aboard the ship. "Doors closed!" yelled Victor. The doors didn't close fast enough. Three vampires made it aboard. Victor shot from the hip. Two burst into flames. Victor rolled off the back of Nightfire and with one sword slice straight down, the remaining vampire fell into flame and dust. They were safe for the moment.

"Rocket One, all power prepare for liftoff!"

"Yes Victor." The voice over the com link replied.

Victor secured Nightfire. "Here, sit," Victor ordered the humans pointing to a bench in the cargo bay. "Belt up. This might get a little bumpy."

CHAPTER SIX

"THREE, TWO, ONE, IGNITION ROCKET One. We have liftoff. Plot coordinates for Nightfire One."

"Yes Victor."

"Mission Support, I have three human passengers. Female adult, female child and male child."

"Copy that Victor."

"Nightfire One."

"Yes Victor."

"Load imploding missile for Valgor."

"Yes Victor. Minus ten minutes, four seconds until docking sequence."

"Thanks Nightfire One. Mission Support, we need to do health workups on the humans once they are aboard Nightfire One."

"Copy that Victor."

"Minus six minutes until docking sequence," Nightfire One informed Victor.

Victor still had to find out how Contessa had made it off the planet with her human, and where did they go.

"One minute until docking sequence," the countdown continued.

"Okay Nightfire One. You have the controls."

"Yes Victor."

Once Nightfire One was locked onto Rocket One and began the docking process, Victor headed to cargo bay one to retrieve the humans and Nightfire.

"Nightfire One."

"Yes Victor. Mission Support P.E.C. five minutes Victor."

"Copy. Make ready."

With Nightfire secured Victor brought the humans to the command module. "Sit down and get belted up. What are your names?"

The woman spoke first. "My name is Susan Gilles. This is Justin."

The little girl was crying and Victor tried to reassure her. "You're alright now. You are going to be okay." As he spoke he thought he could see some of her fear subside. "What's your name?"

"Kala. My name is Kala!"

"You will be home soon, okay Kala?" She nodded and stopped crying. "Thatta girl", Victor said with a smile.

"Mission Support?"

"Yes Victor."

"Watch for any anomalies around Earth's atmosphere. Look for electrically charged particles. Contessa got away."

"Yes Victor. We copy that."

"Nightfire One."

"Yes Victor."

"As soon as Nightflight process begins, launch imploding missiles."

"Copy Victor. Imploding missiles in two minutes and counting. Nightflight in two minutes and thirty seconds."

Victor belted into the cockpit of Nightfire One. "Full view, planet Valgor", he ordered. The image came up on the view finder.

Mission Support began a countdown. "Ten, nine, eight, seven, six, five, four, three, two, one, missiles away. Thirty seconds to impact Victor. Starting P.E.C. Nightflight in thirty seconds."

There was a blue flash on the planet and then it was gone. Nothing was left except a black hole on time and space. In the next moment Nightfire One sat in Earth's orbit. "Nightflight complete. Welcome home Victor."

"It's good to be home. Let's transport these humans to Earth."

"Yes Victor. Right away. We also need to get the herd and Nightfire back to San Diego."

Susan Gilles, a stay at home mom from Salem, Oregon had been abducted two weeks earlier and she explained how she had awakened inside a small box with no visible sides from the inside. She explained that it was clear and she could see space moving past her until she had arrived at Valgor. Vampires had dumped the boxes into the concrete building like mice in a cage.

Jonathan was already there and the children were brought later. Altogether there were eight humans to start with, and the vampires would come and take one or two at a time.

"We were food. Sometimes they would eat the person right there in front of us. It was horrifying."

"Well, you're safe now," was all Victor could say.

The two children had the same story as Susan. As much as their young minds would allow. The clear box was a transport cage. Victor knew, if he could find one of the boxes he would have his answer. That would also answer how the vampires travelled through space.

Back at Mission Support, Professor McCall was attending to Rocket One. "Those vamps really did a job on the outside of the vessel."

"Yes we were lucky to get out alive," Victor said.

"Yes. I'm very glad to see you back safe."

"And I'm really glad to see you Lori."

They stood and looked at one another for a moment. Victor turned and said, "I have work to do with the cattle."

Lori McCall knew there was a lot of work to do but she could not help think that she had fallen in love with Victor. It was something Victor had known for some time.

CHAPTER SEVEN

VICTOR WAS WORKING IN THE holding pen with the cattle. He was injecting blood from Nightfire into the bovine. The idea was to get the Lipenstein's rare blood to be hosted in the cattle then feed the cattle to the vampires. Contessa had said the cure was in the big stallion's blood and Alu had been very excited about Nightfire's blood. Also, Victor had studied the purebred's blood along with other purebreds such as dogs and cats. His conclusion was that only equines had a dominant cellular genetic makeup even stronger than that of the vampires. But only the purest of breeds had the trait; Arabians, Lipensteins, and the Nordic Clydesdales, a giant of a horse from Norway.

Contessa wanted all of them dead so vampires could live forever. It had been eight hundred and fifty years since the vampires had killed Nightfire's mother and Victor's brother Jose'. It was back in France on the horse farm where Victor had become a vampire. Until now there had been a lot of battles and a lot of wars. Death and mayhem had become the only thing Victor knew, but this might work. This may be the answer to all of the blood that had been shed for thousands of years.

"Conrad?"

"Yes Victor."

"Any luck on finding those electric impulses I had asked about?"

"We are working on it Victor. It seems that there are a lot of those specific particles. We even determined that there were some of these cubes in space. There are some on Mars, our moon, even as far out as the galaxy's edge."

"Okay Conrad. I need exact coordinates for a cube that is close by."

"I can do better than that. I have a list of all the cubes we have found so far."

"Okay Conrad, copy that. As soon as I am finished here at the holding pens I will be right there and Conrad, give out the coordinates of the cubes and have everybody stay away from them. I believe they are some kind of snare or traps for humans."

"Copy that Victor."

The first cube Victor was going to look at was only a short mile and a half from Mission Support, just outside San Diego's safety perimeter due south. Victor arrived at the exact location of the coordinates. He saw nothing but the electromagnetic meter said different. They were invisible. How close could you be before you were trapped Victor wondered?

As it turned out they were not traps at all, but transport cages. Victor found one and examined it. They were three feet square and you could see out, but could not see in. The plan was now to put something alive inside and follow the electrical impulse trail back to from wherever it had come. Victor hoped that would be Contessa Vargas. He had decided not to remove the cube but instead place one of his smaller purebred calves inside one. This calf was also a host to the pure blood.

"Conrad?"

"Yes Victor?"

"We need to set up tracking on this cube to wherever it goes."

"Copy Victor."

"Professor McCall?"

"Yes Victor."

"Rocket One and Nightfire One. How long until they are operational?"

"You can have Nightflight in forty five minutes."

"Okay, I will be there in thirty minutes."

Victor returned to the holding pens with Nightfire and retrieved the calf. He laid it across the saddle and rode hard back to the cube. "Conrad are you ready?"

"Yes Victor. Whenever you are."

Victor placed the calf inside the cube. It immediately closed around the calf and large sparks of electricity began to whip around the cube and then it was gone. "Conrad did you get that?"

"Yes Victor. We are tracking it."

Victor rode Nightfire hard back to Mission Support. Dr. McCall was there waiting. "Rocket One is ready when you are Victor."

"Thanks Lori."

He loaded Nightfire aboard the rocket ship and made his way to the cockpit. "Conrad, how's the tracking coming?"

"Good Victor. It looks like it headed toward Saturn alright. I will lock in coordinates when it stops."

Victor took over. "Rocket One set for launch in five, four, three, two, ignition. We have lift off. Rocket One docking with Nightfire One in three minutes and counting." A short silence and then he resumed, "Two minutes, fifty nine seconds. It's a clean burn. Nightfire One you have the controls."

"Yes Victor."

Conrad's excited voice came on the com. "Victor the cube has stopped. It is on the opposite side of Saturn. As best we can tell it is on a small asteroid and the calf is not alone."

"Copy that. Lay in coordinates for one hundred miles away from the asteroid."

"That's pretty close Victor."

Dr. Bell's voice cautioned.

"It will be fine Conrad. We are losing precious time. If that asteroid is a ship it may leave before I arrive."

"Copy that."

"Docking in one minute." Rocket One started its final approach to Nightfire One. In ten, nine, eight,…Victor had confidence in Nightfire One. Two trips in as many days. Docking complete Victor. Start countdown to P.E.C. Nightflight in Ten, nine, eight, seven, six,…

"Conrad?"

"Yes Victor."

"Good work as always to the crew and staff at Mission Support."

"Our prayers are with you Victor. God speed."

Two, one, Nightflight! In the blink of an eye Victor had ridden the very fabric of space itself to the outermost rings of Saturn. "Nightflight complete Victor," came the synthesized voice.

"Thanks Nightfire One. Laser cannons ready on my mark."

"Yes Victor." The voice came over his com link switching seamlessly. "Amorphic parameter not suitable for human or vampires. However there are humans and vampires on the asteroid."

"Copy Nightfire One. Looks like I will be suiting up for this one."

Victor went to the armory where the weapons and environmental space suits were kept. Ten minutes later, Victor boarded a small two man shuttle that would carry him to the asteroids surface and back. Only the laser pistols and some light grenades would be taken. Additional firepower would come from Nightfire One. Victor made his decent to the asteroid which would take ten minutes. He asked, "Nightfire One? How many?"

"There are three humans, fourteen vampires, and one bovine."

"Lock in on their coordinates."

"Yes Victor."

"Heads up laser targeting and set one imploding missile for our exit."
"Yes Victor."

As Victor got close to the asteroid he could see several structures. The shuttle set down five hundred feet from the first structure. Although walking was difficult, Victor's environmental suit provided additional gravity to compensate for any differences that might occur. This made moving much easier. Victor made his way to the first structure, a small concrete block with airtight windows. The entrance was a large tube with an air lock. Entry would equal the atmosphere of Earth. He went in and twenty seconds later he was able to remove his helmet. The entry door opened soon after. He stepped inside the small room which only had a stairway leading down. Victor left his helmet on the floor by the door of the air lock and started down the stairway.

"Nightfire One."

"Yes Victor."

"Heads up view."

"Yes Victor."

Moments later the viewer showed multiple levels with a larger room at the bottom with a series of tunnels leading off it. On the thirteenth level Victor's viewfinder picked up two fast moving vamps. As soon as they were in sight his two head shots connected. They burst into flames. Three more vamps were moving up fast. Victor got off one shot, but two were on him. As the first one reached him he turned slightly to the right. The vampire overshot him by inches. The second vamp hit Victor head on but he was able to stick the laser pistol under the vampires face and pulled the trigger. Victor jumped and threw a backward scissor kick catching the first vampire in the neck at the base of the skull. The vamps face was smashed into the wall. When the vampire bounced off the wall, Victor used his momentum to drive him into the step. Victor stomped down on the front of his throat and pinched his head off. 'Kind of like putting out a cigarette', Victor thought.

The viewfinder showed it was clear to the room at the bottom. As Victor reached the bottom room he could smell death and old stale blood. This was certainly a death chamber for humans. Two tunnels headed eastward. 'More than likely to the other structures,' Victor thought. It had only been a few hundred yards away.

As Victor made his way down the first tunnel the same glowing rocks or crystals as he found on Valgor were lighting up as he came close to them. Victor thought to himself, 'Wherever the rocks are from, so were the vampires.' This because of the color of the stones was the same color as the vampires' skin. Victor also noticed bovine feces and the smell of the calf. It had been lead along this tunnel not too long ago.

Soon Victor came to the end of the first tunnel. It opened up into a larger chamber that was round with a stairway leading upward to a large doorway.

Victor made his way up the stairs and as he opened the door he was hit with a thundering blow to his right temple.

Victor was out cold. It felt like he had been hit with a tree! He awoke with the searing pain of his leg being broken by the force of being whirled like a rag doll. The whole room was spinning and the sound of vampires screeching was deafening. Victor could feel the leg close to being ripped off. The force of being whipped about was unbearable. He knew somehow he had to focus. The grenades! If he could reach a grenade! But the centrifugal force was holding him out like a bull whip. At that moment the vampire let go and there was a loud thud as Victor hit the wall. He felt more bones break, including his left arm, and some ribs on the left side.

Victor was unconscious again for a few seconds. He awoke again from the same pain as the very large vampire was picking him up by the back of the head and neck. Victor could only see bits and pieces as blood was flowing into his eyes. He had no time to focus, only react. Victor's right hand still worked and he fumbled for a grenade, pulled the pin, and tossed it away into the air. Victor felt no pain, only gratification with himself as the light grenade went off and bright UV light filled the chamber. Victor must have seen six or seven vampires light up at once. Brilliant amber light filled the round room almost as if someone had turned on the lights and caught the bad shadow doing bad things.

The heads up view finder in Victor's right eye was simply flashing E, E, E, which meant error. The com link in his left ear had completely quit. Victor wiped at his eyes so he might see. The back half of the calf laid on the floor across from him. That had been the "tree" he had been hit with.

Victors left foot was bent in an odd angle. First the arm. Victor placed his arm between his thighs and pulled back as hard as he could. The arm snapped and crackled as he did so. He could also feel his ribs pop back into their proper places. Victor laid there for a moment to catch his breath. Now came the daunting task of getting the leg turned back around. But which way to turn it? To the right it felt like jelly. It turned very easily then fell over to one side. The bone was broken in many places. Victor had his left foot in place against the wall with his right foot and then pushed with the right side of his body. This had the effect of straightening the leg's bones into place. The old vampire felt as if he was sweating bullets but it was mostly just blood. His own blood.

His body had begun to repair itself, but it would be a long while for everything to be back to normal...Well, as normal as it can be for an eight hundred and fifty year old vampire. There was not much time. Victor somehow had to pick himself up and get moving. He crawled to what was left of the calf and tore a strip of hide from it. He then broke off the calf's leg at the bottom and tied it to his own for support. It wasn't a very good splint, but it was better than nothing.

Victor crawled then hobbled back through the tunnel. As he entered the larger room at the bottom of the stairway he noticed the crystal rock in the second tunnel had been lit. Victor could sense humans and maybe a vampire. They were several flights up on the stairway. He hurried as fast as he could, which was not fast at all. As he reached the room with the air lock, the door was already closed and filling with the outside atmosphere. He couldn't tell who was who in their space suits.

Victor quickly found his helmet and attached it. The vampire and its party of humans were already out of the air lock and moving across the surface of the asteroid in a westward direction. As Victor entered the air lock and it began to let the outside atmosphere in, he noticed there was a tear in his suit and it was only holding twenty five percent oxygen. He would have to make a run for the shuttle. There was no time to pursue the vampires. Victor was operating on one leg and one arm at best, and no communications with Nightfire One or Mission Support.

Five hundred yards seemed like five miles. His oxygen was depleted and there was still sixty yards to go. Victors mind began playing tricks on him. He first thought he was playing at his home in France, with his sister and brother on a warm and sunny day. He could hear their laughter and see the sunlight through Jewels' hair and Jose smiled in his face. Victor ran into the shuttle and fell back. Back to reality. He closed the door and the cockpit automatically re-pressurized. He removed the helmet with a gasp!

"Power on!" He gasped. "Nightfire One!"

"Yes Victor."

"Where are the humans?"

"Due west of here Victor."

"Nightfire One. My heads up targeting is off line!"

"Yes Victor, along with your com link. Also you have sustained some damage to your body parts."

"Yes, yes Nightfire One. The humans! What about the humans?!"

"It looks as if they are headed for an energy cube, a rather large one."

"On your mark Nightfire One, target the cube with laser cannons!"

"Copy Victor."

Several light beams lit up the surface of the asteroid, then there was a bright flash.

"The cube is destroyed Victor."

The shuttle lifted off the asteroid and headed due west. There they were. A small group of humans and one vampire.

"Nightfire One, target the structures. Laser cannon. Fire at will."

"Yes Victor." Came the response, and in a few moments the structure was destroyed.

"Nightfire One."

"Yes Victor."

"Open com link to the space suits."

"Com links open."

"Hello Victor!" The familiar voice answered.

"Hello Contessa. You bringing your lunch with you?"

"You might say that. Victor, that was very smart of you to send the bovine and then to follow it to us. Victor, these humans feasted on the bovine. You have the cure don't you? The cure for vampirism!? They were vampires Victor, now they are humans. It only took minutes for them to be cured, but these humans *wanted* to be vampires. Great vampires like Alu and me! Here Victor, let me show you."

With that the humans lifted the visors on their helmets. Victor's heart began to race and his eyes blinked rapidly. Had he lost too much blood or was this some kind of trick Contessa was pulling?

"Yes Victor, it is as you see it." *The fi rst humans face was Jose', his brother*! "I went back that cold and rainy day to reclaim his body. You had already reattached the head. My job was easy after that. The process is the same if your victim is dead or alive."

The second face Victor saw was of his beloved baby sister Jewels, but not exactly. Something wasn't quite right. "It is her Victor! It is Jewels your sister!"

Victor could feel his throat begin to close up and his eyes start to cloud from the tears.

"Well, it is mostly her anyway Victor! The task of finding Jewels a new skin from top to bottom was not so easy. You remember, we tore her old one off! Haha! But after a few weeks I finally convinced her that his one would do just fine. Besides, who needs to endure all that pain of constantly trying on new skin." As Contessa spoke, Jewels was smiling a sick twisted smile as her body swayed back and forth.

Tears were streaming in and around Victors eyes. Eight hundred-fifty years and he had never cried. Now he felt so much pain he thought he may lose his mind. As the third vampire stood in the light so Victor could better see. The small landing craft was almost out of control. Victor was so focused on the humans that piloting the shuttle was almost impossible. His mind was beginning to shut down at what he was seeing. The third one was Kendra Collingsworth, his beloved. Kendra was as beautiful as she had ever been. Her name slipped from his lips as would a leaf from a tree in late fall, or as winters first snowflake. "Kendra..."

"Yes my love. It is I."

"But how?" Victor said with all of his breath, a whisper of what dead life he had left in his soul. The shuttle bounced from right to left.

Contessa spoke. "Kendra's heart is from a young whore from Charleston's waterfront. After the old man blew the other out her chest, I had to find a suitable one to replace it. And she has done very well over the centuries. Very well with that face...especially that body...but her new heart has allowed her to keep very, *very busy.*

Kendra laughed aloud at Contessa's comment. "AND I WILL LOVE YOU TOO!", Kendra bellowed!

Victors mind went blank and he swooned in grief for a few seconds. When he awoke in the shuttle it was quiet and still. Control of the shuttle was his first thought. It did not respond. "Victor" a voice exclaimed, "Its Conrad Victor."

"Mission Support. Nightfire One has control of the shuttle. What... where did Contessa and all the humans go?"

"Due west."

"Are you alright Victor? Come back to Nightfire One."

"Yes, I will be alright. Release the controls Nightfire One."

"Yes Victor."

Victor brought the shuttle around in front of the vampires and her party of dead. They were nothing more than revenge on Victor. "Imploding missile. Entire asteroid."

"Yes Victor. On your mark."

"Laser cannons, target five on asteroid surface."

"On your mark Victor."

Whimpers came from the space suits. "Please Victor! I love you! Please don't do this Victor! We love you!"

"STOP IT CONTESSA!" Victor yelled, NO MORE SICK GAMES! NO MORE MIND CONTROL! THESE GAMES YOU PLAY ARE OVER! The ones I love are in heaven! The one's you love are in hell! TIME TO GO BE WITH THEM!"

The sound of the light cutting through the thin, toxic atmosphere was deathly, as Victor was only a few yards away. Victor stared into their eyes... their dead eyes. A flash, and then only dust. Victor remained just staring into space as he remembered his family and Kendra as they were.

Conrad Bells voice came on the com link. "Victor! Victor! Are you alright? Victor?"

"Yes. I will be okay. Nightfire One, you have the controls."

"Yes Victor."

"Conrad, prepare to load the other cubes with bovines. Let's begin to take back our planet and our universe."

"Yes Victor. We will get started right away."

"Nightfire One?"

"Yes Victor."

"Bring the shuttle aboard."

"Yes Victor."

CHAPTER EIGHT

"PLOT A COURSE FOR EARTH, Nightfire One."

"Yes Victor."

"Mission Support, how long until Nightflight?"

"Three minutes and counting."

"Conrad?"

"Yes Victor?"

"How many cubes have you located?"

"Two hundred or so throughout the universe.

"How many only on Earth?"

"Twenty two."

"Okay, let's get those loaded with bovines at San Diego. The rest will be loaded on Nightfire One for transport into space."

"Copy that Victor. We are all looking forward to seeing you back here at home. Here is Dr. McCall. She wants to talk to you."

Lori McCall's voice came on the com link. "Victor are you hurt badly?"

"No. Nothing that a day or two can't fix."

Nightfire One's synthesized voice interrupted, "Two minutes and counting until Nightflight."

"Victor, I will meet you in the rocket bay."

"Yes I would like to see you too Lori."

"Fifty nine, fifty eight, fifty seven..."

"There's something I would like to discuss with you." Something he should have told her from the first time he saw her. That he loved her. Somehow he felt he could admit it to himself, but not to her.

"Five, four, three, two, Nightflight." The large spacecraft dissolved into the black fabric of space to reappear above Earths stratosphere in no more time than a thought. "Nightflight complete Victor."

"Nightfire and I will see you shortly."

"Rocket One ready for launch in three, two, one, launch." Nightfire One released Rocket One from its moors. "Rocket One, you are cleared for ignition." Small rockets fired. The ship rolled on course for San Diego Mission Support Landing Bay.

The flight took only a few minutes.

Victor addressed the terrestrial flight computers, "Mission Support Docking, you have control."

"Copy that Victor. Welcome home."

The bay doors opened and Rocket One was gently positioned in the docking bay. Victor could see Lori from the windows of Rocket One. Also present was the rest of the staff and crew of Mission Support. They were all waiting to see how badly Victor may have been hurt. The hatch on Rocket One opened. Lori and Conrad rushed in to retrieve Victor but he was already standing by the hatch door. They rushed under his arms to support him.

"Oh thank you Conrad. Can you see that Nightfire is taken to his corral?"

"Yes Victor, of course, right away."

"Victor was very weary. It was all he could do to stand even with help. "Come on Victor, let's get you to the infirmary so you can rest." Said Lori.

Even though Victor's physical body would heal soon, the micro-bionics needed to be repaired. The com link in his left ear continued to bleed as did the view finder in his right eye. That would be Professor McCall's job. If she knew Victor, he would be wanting upgrades.

A few days went by and Victor was almost as good as new, and the new upgraded bionic components were implanted. The new data com link came with upgrades that reduced interruptions in coms. The heads up view finder had a new laser guided targeting system, which was state of the art. Both were built with nano technology with self awareness to constantly upgrade themselves.

"Good morning Victor! How's the new gear?"

"Very nice Lori. You and your team do really good work." Victor changed subjects. "Lori, there is something I want to say to you." She was standing close and examining the implant in his eye. He grabbed her hands and pulled her to him. "Lori, I...I love you. And I have since I first laid eyes on you."

"Well it sure took you long enough to say it! Is it going to take you that long to kiss me too?"

Victor kissed her deeply and for that moment the universe ceased to exist. It was just two souls on a plane of bliss.

"Victor, I have wanted this for so long." Again he kissed her. The room seemed to spin and Lori felt as if she were leaving her body. The emotion was overwhelming as all of her senses were heightened above a human level. Her body began to shake.

Victor pulled her away. "Lori! Look at me!"

She began to come back to herself.

"Lori, are you okay?"

"Yes...more than okay...much more."

Victor smiled. "Lori we still have a lot more work to do."

"Oh...uh...work...yes, work to do." She took a breath and composed herself then leaned in for one more small kiss. Then she turned and said, "Yes. Back to work."

CHAPTER NINE

CONRAD HAD THE CUBES LOADED with bovines. Some of the cubes had already started their journeys. The bovines were specially fitted with homing beacons to track and pinpoint their exact locations and would be used to calculate how many vampires were present. Some of the long range probes would be needed to transmit data back to Mission Support along with scopes placed throughout the galaxies, like security cameras for the universe. This along with hi tech equipment used in tracking electrical impulses anywhere would help them defend their planet from vampires.

Because it was sure, once they figured out their food supply was poisoned they would be coming... Coming hungry and mad. Victor knew the pure bloods would live on but the human vampires would be cured and would decay and die. Knowing about the cubes would make the vamps have to seek out a food supply. And when they came to Earth, the people of Earth would be ready for the infestation of vampires. Ready to eradicate the vermin once and for all.

Victor knew it would not be long before vampires were upon them. Alu had said there were hundreds like him, but he was the father. How much of that was true was still yet to be seen. Satellites for communications were retrofitted with laser cannons and sat quietly around Earth. This would be a battle on Earth as much as in space. Without a food source, vampires would begin to feed upon one another.

All humans would have to be armed with body lasers and sunlight grenades. The new body laser, detected vamps and targeted them for a short burst of light which set the vampire on fire. So far, not enough had been produced but there were plenty of UV grenades. The humans would not go down without one hell of a fight. Just the fact that they were aware of vampires coming was a big advantage.

Any cube could be detected from their electromagnetic impulse. The hope was that the laser cannons would detect the electromagnetic impulse entering our space around Earth, and be intercepted on the spot. Ships that arrived, if any, would be hit with imploding missiles from Earths defenses and from Nightfire One.

Places like San Diego with reinforced security would be used as headquarters for the World Command. All strikes on the vampires would be coordinated through its command centers throughout the world. DEATH TO ALL VAMPIRES would be their battle cry. Mission Support had been tracking the cubes and all had left Earth on their way to parts unknown through the universe. Some went as far as Pluto. Some went as close as our moon. But none had returned.

First an hour passed, then two. Still no cubes had returned. Could it be that all vampires might be the human type? It was unlikely. Suddenly an urgent call shattered the silence.

"WE HAVE INCOMING!" shouted Conrad Bell.

"Auto arm the laser cannons!" Yelled Victor.

All humanity armed themselves, ready to battle for their survival. The vampires were coming.

CHAPTER TEN

THE ELECTROMAGNETIC IMPULSES WERE COMING from every direction throughout the universe. Mission Support was tracking two hundred ninety-two impulses, all with vampire vibrations. Some were starting to enter Earth's atmosphere. Earths defenses came alive. Laser cannons began firing at will, knocking out dozens. Bright lights lit up the sky.

"Direct hits Victor!" The voices sounded on his com link. The battle had begun. Some of the cubes broke off their direct assault and began a criss-cross pattern.

"Nightfire One! Lock and fire at will!"

"Yes Victor," was the quick response. And Nightfire One opened fire with laser cannons and imploding missiles. Its first barrage took out thirty cubes. Some of the cubes pushed their way on to Earth, where they were met by Earth's human force. Some of the vampires were laser blasted. Some were hit with UV grenades. All were taken down. In space there were only a few left. It was like shooting fish in a barrel for Nightfire One. Soon there were no more.

"Conrad! Any signs of vampires?"

"No Victor. No vibrations whatsoever. Except you that is."

They had done it. They had killed all of the vampires! It was too soon to really tell. They would know more in the next few days.

"Copy that Mission Support." It was all over in a matter of a few minutes.

Eight hundred fifty years of death and destruction. It was a path which Victor had been on for his own eternity. Old and dying vampires that were now cured of the curse of vampirism were leaving messages for the living. Most were asking for forgiveness from the rest of mankind. But it was not necessary because only a few had actually wanted to become vampires. Now their dying bodies began to fill the streets. Millions had been infected. They would all have to be burned or buried. The fires would last for months and entire cities would have to be buried. The toll on Earth was immeasurable. Maybe a million humans total had survived uninfected. It wasn't many considering there were over six billion just a few years before.

The com link was silent. The universe seemed still. No motion, no noise, just light from faraway stars and suns in other galaxies. Victor couldn't help but think there was other life out in deep space, and much of that life was affected by love or vampirism. He couldn't be sure. All he did know was that Earth had a chance now. Even with its own small differences it had a chance. Humans had a new start; a new beginning free of madness and free of the fear of vampirism. Still the task before them was great.

Now it was just Nightfire, a few bovines and himself; The only ones infected with the curse of the vampire. Victor had known this day would come where he might be the only vampire still carrying the blood of the vampires and Victor always had said, "All vampires must die". He pondered those thoughts for a moment. Victor had always liked Montana. Butte particularly, and now his thoughts drifted to his home.

Then he thought to himself, 'You never know when a vampire may need killing, or if one might have slipped through somewhere.' He considered if it might be best to stick around for a while.

"Conrad. Let's bring Rocket One home."

"Yes Victor. Right away."

Victor made his way to the Rocket. Nightfire One would be left in orbit for scientific purposes and the defense of Earth. Maybe Victor would take the giant ship on other explorations into deep space.

The rocket made its way back to Mission Support on Earth. Victor exited the craft and walked across the hanger. Not many humans were present, but a few. Some smiled, some shook his hand and thanked him. Most were busy with the everyday war that was now ending. He made his way to the holding pen where the bovines and Nightfire were kept. Victor let himself in and walked to the great stallion. The two looked at one another for a long moment. Victor thought, How did the black stallion feel about living so long? Was his soul tired? What was it that kept him from going mad? Was it revenge like himself or a sense of loyalty to Victor? Whatever it was he was glad that Nightfire had been on the journey along with him. As Victor stroked Nightfire's neck and mane, he asked himself the same questions.

But right now he had a long cattle drive to attend to. He moved the small herd north to his home in Montana. The trip would only seem like a few days to Victor. The drive was something he needed to reconnect with himself. He also needed to survey the land along the way to see what damage the millenniums of vampirism had rendered across it. He spent many years to go into space, but right now the only space he needed was the space between San Diego and Butte Montana.

CHAPTER ELEVEN

"ALRIGHT COWBOY. LET'S GET THIS cattle up to Montana."

Victor turned to see Lori McCall sitting in the saddle behind him on a gray mare, and a red sorrel pack horse tethered behind. She nudged the mare up beside him and reached out then pulled Victor toward her. "Victor, I am ready to start the rest of our lives together." And then she kissed him with a long deep kiss until they started to laugh from the applause of a small crowd that had gathered.

Professor Bell spoke. "Victor, we all are going to miss you. And Lori you also. We just wanted to thank you for what you have done for the human race. We will go on with greater humanity, cherishing our lives that you have fought for. We will never forget you Victor."

"Lori and I will be back Conrad. There is still a lot of work to be done, and humans should work to make the Earth whole again. It will be much easier without the fear of vampires ruling the world. The ones that went before us, our loved ones, friends and families did not die in vain."

As they released the bovines from the holding pen, and slowly moved them north the crowd roared with cheers.

A short four months later just outside of Butte Montana the small herd started down into a little grassy valley.

"Oh Victor it's beautiful! I had no idea!" Exclaimed Lori.

"Yes, it is very beautiful but it's nothing compared to you...As far as being beautiful that is."

At the end of the valley sat a large log cabin that overlooked the valley. It had been a long time since Victor had been here and would be a labor of love for the next few months. Victor knew as did Lori that their life would not be normal but they were in love and that was all that mattered at this point. Even though Victor was a vampire, and Lori was human they would live their lives; Lori as a human, and Victor as a vampire.

In the future the two might travel back to San Diego and back into space. Victor thought that perhaps Lori would enjoy space travel, and the exploration of distant planets.

The thought of Lori having children hadn't even been talked about and the more Victor thought of it, the more unfair it seemed to Lori. After all, she was a beautiful and intelligent woman with her whole human life ahead of her. What would a human and a vampire bring as an offspring? Victor had been fighting eight-hundred fifty years to rid the world of vampires. To propagate offspring; to start a new race of vampires would be wrong. Lori also knew that this wouldn't work, but she didn't want to leave Victor.

To love someone and not be able to touch them would be hard to do, but Victor loved Lori this much. They could live together and work together in a strictly platonic relationship. He didn't know if this would work or not but it was something he was willing to try. Lori had agreed to the terms of the agreement, and in her heart she knew it was the right thing to do.

The two rode up to the corral. Victor dismounted and opened the gate as Lori drove the small herd in. "Leave the horses", said Victor, "I will put them in the barn in a little while."

The two made their way into the log house which seemed a lot bigger up close. A large fireplace first caught Lori's eye. It was built of large rocks and towered through the ceiling of the great room and had a large tree trunk with one flat side for a mantle. A pine wood stair case circled up to the second floor landing which then lead to a guest room and a master bedroom. Both were rustic and elegant.

"Did you build this house?" Lori asked, amazed.

"Yes, it took a couple of years. But yeah."

"It's amazing. I can see why you love it so much here."

"It is my island of solitude. The nearest neighbor is fifteen miles away as the crow flies."

He changed subjects. "Well, make yourself at home. Feel free to look around all you want. When I come back we will get a fire going and rustle up something to eat."

"Okay, that sounds good." Lori said.

Victor left to tend to the horses and Lori made her way upstairs to look around. There were some very old things in the house. Swords on the wall; a lot of them. Possibly a collection she wondered?

There were pictures of people and places a long time past. One painting in particular caught her eye. It was of an older man and his family; his wife, daughter and two sons. Which one was Victor? He looked a little younger, but not much. A picture of a happier time. A good part of Victors life, she thought. How much of his life must have been spent alone, angry and sad? Always contemplating sweet revenge on vampires or perhaps dying; For that moment of peace which would be allowed at life's final release.

There would be no soul searching for Victor, for his soul had long since gone. But the question hadn't been answered in Victors case, where? Did The Devil have it, or was God holding onto it? She didn't know. What she did know, was that she was deeply in love with Victor, and her life with him was going to be the best she could make of it.

Lori made her way back down to the great room. Victor came through the door with a large tree trunk on his shoulder and placed it in the fireplace.

"Wow", Lori commented, "that looks like you brought the whole tree!" "Yes. It should burn through the night just fine."

"No, I mean, you were carrying a whole tree!" She said in amazement.

"Oh yeah, I guess it's a vampire thing."

"Go vampire!" said Lori with a smile.

Victor returned the smile.

After a while Victor had the light on and dinner cooking. Lori set the table which looked out the window of the dining room. Tonight it looked out over a moonlit grassy valley, frost in color as it was bathed in moonlight. Victor brought in the food. Roasted pheasant he had shot earlier. Fresh wild lettuce with raspberry and chopped black walnuts. It was mostly for Lori who was an avowed vegetarian.

Lori lit the candles on the table. Victor returned with a bottle of wine. 1912 Rayno Pinard. "This is from outside my home town. I hope it is still good." He wondered aloud as he popped the cork. He filled the two glasses almost full. "The smell is good anyway."

Lori covered her pallet with the vintage wine. "Oh Victor, it tastes wonderful!"

"Good. I knew I was keeping it for the best of times." He said as he held up his glass to salute her. "To beautiful company. The wine makes the journey across your beautiful lips of which I am sure, it is not worthy.

"Why Victor Jane. You are a charmer!"

He smiled. "I think not my queen. Only a willing slave to your love." They both laughed out loud. "You're funny," said Lori.

"And you're very beautiful."

He moved to her side of the table and bent down and kissed her lightly on the lips. She pressed back harder as their fire of passion arose from within. He picked her up from the chair and as they stared deep into each other's eyes they seemed to float up the stairs to the master bedroom.

"I guess that whole 'platonic thing' is off?" Victor grinned.

"Yeah. I'm pretty sure that's what this means." Said Lori returning his smile. Then she said enthusiastically, "Go human!"

The End